The Leavetaking

by Anna Blauveldt

Cover photograph used with permission and licencing agreement with JJWenzeliMages © 2022
https://www.jjwenzelimages.com/
Cover Model: Claudine Vivian

Editor-in-Chief: Michel Weatherall

The Leavetaking, 2022, Published by Broken Keys Publishing
brokenkeypublishing@gmail.com

Published November 2022
First Printing

Dedication

To Nicole, Catherine, Molly, Marie-Hélène, Pauline, Susan, and Iola, dear friends whose strength and generosity inspire me every day.

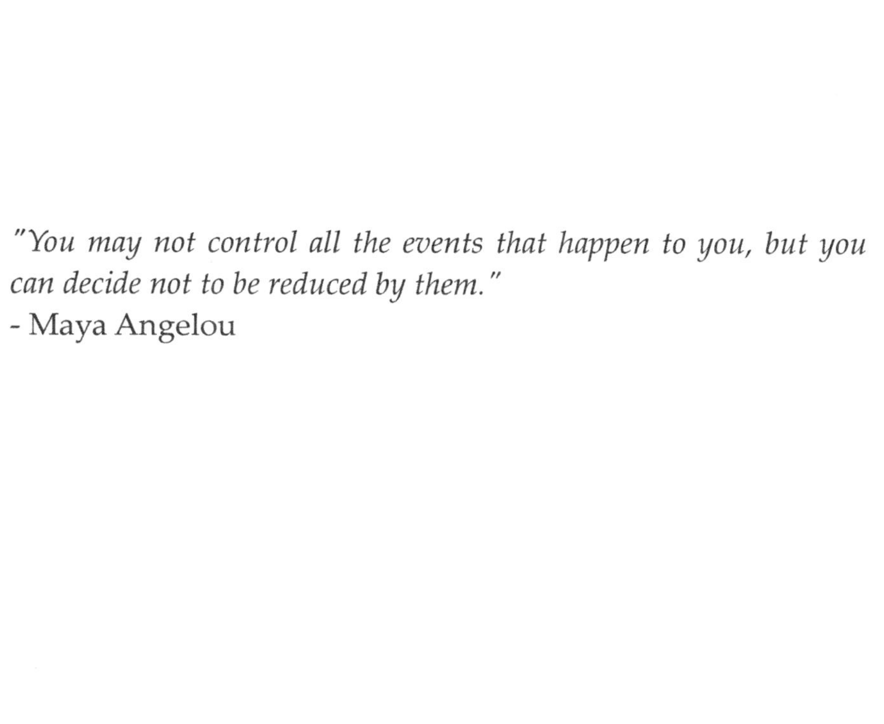

"You may not control all the events that happen to you, but you can decide not to be reduced by them."

\- Maya Angelou

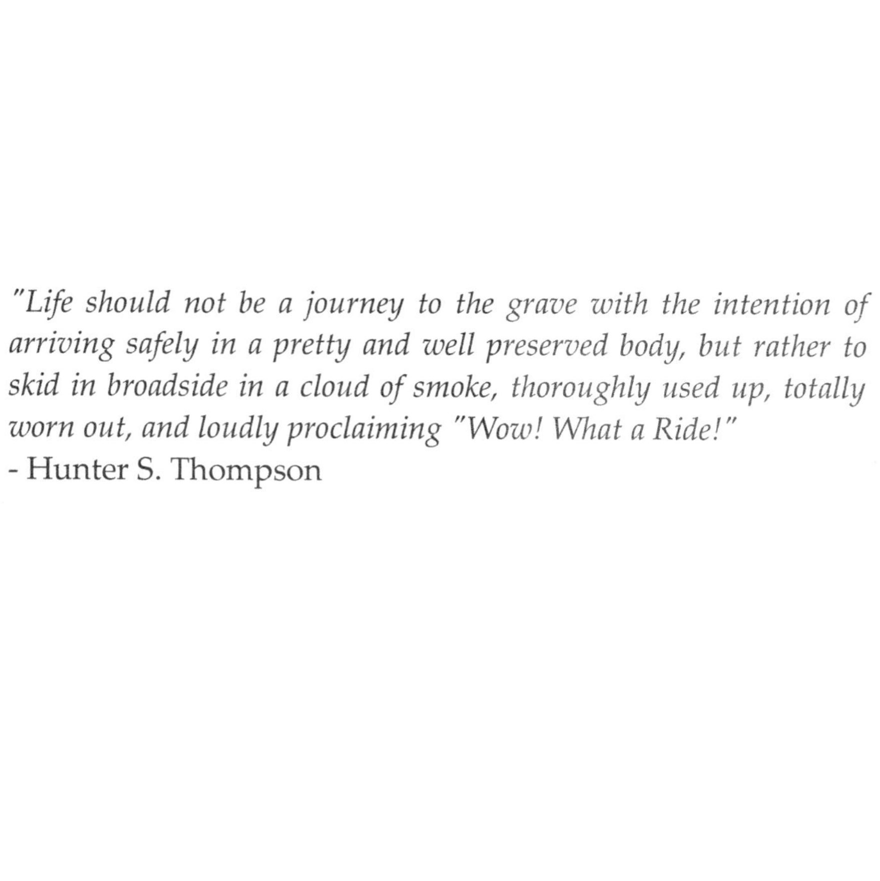

"Life should not be a journey to the grave with the intention of arriving safely in a pretty and well preserved body, but rather to skid in broadside in a cloud of smoke, thoroughly used up, totally worn out, and loudly proclaiming "Wow! What a Ride!"
- Hunter S. Thompson

"Destiny is a worrying concept. I don't want to be fated, I want to choose."

- Jeanette Winterson

Chapter One

Hurtling west in the centre lane of the Queensway, Molly Bustin's mind went completely blank. She tried everything not to panic. Yoga breathing. Loose-shaking her shoulders. Humming 'Imagine' along with the classic rock station. Nothing worked. Her hands were frozen on the wheel and her stomach was a sour simmering mess.

Where the hell am I going? And why? The questions played over and over again in a loop in her head. If she repeated them often enough, maybe they'd break through the wall between her and her memory.

Molly was doing well over a hundred when she finally took her foot off the gas. It was a mistake. Seconds later, even the cars in the slow lane were going faster than she was. Then came a sharp horn blast from the vehicle behind. She checked the rear-view mirror. The scowling driver was tailgating her back bumper, five feet away at most, and flipping her the bird. On top of that, hot tears filling her eyes made it hard to see the road ahead.

There was no choice now. She had to get off the highway. Molly flicked on her right-turn signal and carefully edged the Volvo across two lanes, past construction barriers at the Bronson off-ramp, to take the next exit. Parkdale. She knew this part of the city well. A friend of hers used to live around here. What was her name again? Diane? Debbie?

"Get a GRIP!" she scolded herself. Why try to think of someone's name from the dim past when she couldn't even remember why she'd just been speeding along an eight-lane thoroughfare at the start of rush hour?

She finally found a space to pull over in a no-parking zone on a leafy side street near the Civic Hospital. Molly was still trembling as she turned off the ignition. She didn't give a damn if the parking control officer, strutting from car to car dispensing tickets with a smug grin on his face, gave her one too. She wasn't moving until she could think straight.

Eyes closed, she rested her head on the steering wheel.

What in God's name is happening to me?Am I losing my mind or what?

It took ten minutes before Molly felt calm enough to drive again.

This wasn't just a one-off memory lapse. There'd been other times lately when it failed her. Why, just this Easter, she forgot the name of Carrie's husband. Totally unremarkable, Jeremy was, in her view. . . his name *was* Jeremy, wasn't it? He was the kind of person who always sat wordless on the fringes of family gatherings, a piece of furniture in human form. Like one of those fancy accent chairs, he was nice to look at, but basically only filled an empty space. Molly never understood what her daughter saw in him. Still, he'd been her son-in-law for more than a decade and she should have been able to remember his name. At the time, it was mildly embarrassing. She didn't think all that much about it afterward. Until today.

And then there were the migraines she'd been having lately in the mornings, when it felt like her brain was trying to punch its way through the top of her skull. The Tylenols she took didn't help. She just had to wait out the pain, sitting on the edge of the bathtub in case she needed to throw up in the toilet. It happened more often than not.

This episode on the highway was more troubling, and way more dangerous. Maybe she should give up and follow her husband's advice. Gabe wanted her to go see Dr. Flanagan and arrange to take some tests. He was probably right. She'd make an appointment as soon as she got home.

Parking Ticket Guy was two cars away now. As hard as Molly tried to remember where she was supposed to be going, it just wasn't coming to her. And when he tucked a ticket under the windshield wiper of the SUV ahead, she knew she was next.

It was time to go home. She started the engine, shifted the gear stick into 'Drive' and pulled away. Then she took the long, slow route back through congested streets to where she lived in the Glebe neighbourhood. There was no way she'd risk driving on the Queensway again.

Back in her laneway, she checked her cellphone for messages. It was her friend Hope's text that tweaked her memory. They were supposed to meet, for the first time in ages, at a new outdoor café. Socially distanced, of course.

Where r u? Hope asked. *Did something happen? R u okay?*

So sorry, Molly texted back. *Ran out of gas.*

* * *

Two months later, Molly was on a quest to buy marijuana.

The last time she'd smoked weed had been over forty years ago. Back then it was illegal, of course, but who *didn't* smoke up in university in the 70s? And hash. Molly did that too, more than a few times. Even so, she was one of the more cautious students in her dorm. For the more adventurous, dropping acid was a frequent recreational sport. That was a vice too far for Molly. After her roommate Willa saw giant snakes and Dali-esque melting sidewalks on a nightmare three-hour trip, Molly drew the line at LSD.

These days, possession of marijuana was legal. Since 2018, people could even grow their own, up to four cannabis plants per household. Molly had no intention of doing that. Too much of a commitment to the stuff. She just wanted a few joints for one very special occasion: her sixty-fifth birthday on the Labour Day weekend, two weeks away.

She had invited her oldest friends from her university days to help her celebrate it at the Chateau Bord-du-Lac resort. They had something else to celebrate, too. It was the first time since they'd all had their COVID vaccinations that they could actually get together in person. No need to Zoom this time. Three of them – Molly, Beth and Hope – hadn't been in the same room since the pandemic started in early 2020, well over a year before. And it had been much longer than that for Willa. She moved to Vancouver right after graduation and hadn't been back since. Molly thought smoking pot at their getaway would be a sentimental salute to their four misspent years together.

Her destination that day, the *Northern de-Lights* dispensary, was one of dozens of cannabis shops in the city. Located in a trendy west-end shopping district of upscale boutiques and cafés, it was sandwiched between an independent bookstore on one side and an antique shop on the other.

It was hardly an opium den in a red-light district. And it wasn't like she was a desperate heroin addict about to make an illicit back-alley transaction. So why did she feel just a touch uncomfortable going there?

At first hesitating to enter, Molly pretended to inspect the oak secretary desk on the sidewalk in front of the antique shop. It had a hand-written 'Marked Down' sign perched on top, but she wasn't the slightest bit interested. She already had one like it at home. It was a stalling tactic, opening and closing the drawers, while she worked up the nerve to take those last few steps. Just as the antique shop clerk approached her hoping to make a sale, Molly shook her head, backed away from the desk, and entered the *Northern de-Lights* shop.

What she saw made her feel more at ease.

Brightly lit by shabby-chic crystal chandeliers, with granite-and-wrought-iron display counters and engineered barn board walls, the place could easily be offering essential oils or fancy imported cheeses. It was the half-dozen potted cannabis plants scattered around the shop that made it clear what was on offer. There were a couple of customers inside. They appeared to be in their late twenties. Not the current crop of hippy wannabes but, by their appearance, geeks of the Best Buy kind, a species familiar to Molly because it included her software engineer son, Cam.

She could do this.

According to his name tag, it was Zeke the 'Concierge' who served her, and he was well informed. Perhaps too well informed. It turned out this wasn't going to be a straightforward purchase. Zeke showed her over a dozen different strains of cannabis pre-rolls, with flavour descriptions sounding like those applied to fine wines. 'Earthy', 'citrus', 'peppery', even 'pine.' Who would want to smoke anything that tasted like pine? Molly wondered.

It didn't take long for her to be overwhelmed by choice. She had no idea there were so many varieties. Back in the day, it was easy: whatever the contents of any joint passed her way, she toked. Eventually, Molly decided on the citrus-flavoured one. A Sativa strain pre-roll three-pack. $27.00.

It was almost inevitable that, as she left *Northern de-Lights* with her artfully wrapped package tucked away in her tote bag, thoughts of her grass-smoking college days came to mind. Life was so simple then, with no worries beyond boys and her studies, in that order. Especially no health worries, unlike now.

After the scary incident on the highway, she'd gone to the doctor to find out what was wrong with her brain. The results of her medical imaging tests were due back any day. She'd have to deal with them when the time came, but not now. Now, she was in full nostalgia mode, fondly reminiscing about her carefree past. It was a moment of delicious distraction, and it was soon gone. Molly sighed. 'Silly old woman,' she said to herself as she climbed in her car and pressed the start button. Still, she asked Alexa to play *China Grove* by the Doobie Brothers on the way home.

* * *

Molly told Gabe about her little shopping adventure later at dinner. She already knew what his reaction would be. Gabe Bustin was the straight-and-narrow type. A recently retired procurement executive with the federal government, he'd always gone to work in a suit and tie, even on casual Fridays. Gabe was the only person Molly knew who actually read the small print in every product warranty or mortgage agreement or insurance policy he came across. And when he ate, he thoroughly chewed each mouthful of food exactly fifteen times. It made for long meals.

That evening, it was prime rib roast beef he chewed and chewed. His favourite. Molly had finished her dinner ten minutes earlier. Now she was sitting back in her chair, taking sips from her second glass of Merlot and waiting for Gabe to finish his. She pulled the pre-roll three-pack out of her pocket and placed it on the dining table beside his plate. Then she counted in her head the last of his chews while she anticipated his response. Twelve. Thirteen. Fourteen. Fifteen.

"What *is* this, Molly?"

Gabe placed his knife and fork at a precise right angle on his plate. He picked the pack up and inspected it, both sides, then dropped it immediately.

"What do you think? It's a pack of grass cigarettes. I bought it at one of those new cannabis shops."

"Jesus! You did *what?* Did anybody see you there?"

"I don't think so. Besides, who cares if they did? It's legal now. You know that."

"*I* care. And so would everybody else we know. Aren't you too old to be smoking marijuana?"

"But that's the whole point, Gabe! I got it for my birthday. I can't think of a better way to celebrate. You know, go a little wild. The girls'll love it. Maybe you and I could try one, too?"

He shook his head violently and shoved the pack further away. Molly sighed.

"C'mon Gabe. Don't be such a stick-in-the-mud!"

Where had the joy gone?

All those years ago, when they started dating in their senior year of university, she found his drive, his self-discipline, appealing. Gabe's single-minded ambition would take him – take *them* – places, she just knew it. And he was blandly handsome in a Harrison Ford kind of way. He certainly had a lot more going for him than most of the other guys in the class of '78.

Molly had assets of her own, too, back then. She was smart, at the top of her English literature class and editor of the university's student newspaper. It didn't hurt that she had a trim figure, blue-grey eyes, and honey-colour hair down to her waist. Gabe was impressed. He thought she was the whole package. They married just two months after graduation.

From the outside looking in, they grew to be the perfect little family. Professional husband and author wife with two adorable children. Their son Cameron came first, then daughter Carrie. In the early days, they lived in a new family-friendly subdivision way out in the suburbs, snug in a row of cookie-cutter starter homes. Identical double garages dominated the view as far as the eye could see on both sides of the street, with humble living quarters hidden away behind each.

As soon as Gabe and Molly could afford it, they moved closer to the city centre. The Glebe was more their style anyway, with avenue after avenue of large Victorian brick houses ripe for renovation by upwardly mobile university grads. "Yuppies" they used to call them then.

Young urban professionals. The Bustins fit right in, but their ideal family image was a mirage.

Gabe's desire to succeed had choked out all traces of passion and spontaneity early in his career, and they never came back. And, even though he lived in the same house as Molly and Cam and Carrie, he was an absentee husband and father, leaving for work every morning at seven o'clock and rarely getting back before eight at night. Sometimes he worked through the weekends, too.

His mid-life crisis in the late '90's, when it became obvious he wasn't going all the way to the top, had been a spectacular flameout. It didn't help that Molly was starting to achieve more success than him with royalties from her children's picture book series. Having two teenagers in the house didn't make things any easier, either. There were escalating arguments and months of too much late-night drinking. And Molly suspected there was an affair. She'd found an asthma inhaler with bright red lipstick on it on the passenger-side floor of their Subaru after one of Gabe's Saturdays at the office. He looked way too flustered when he tried to explain it belonged to a colleague.

A thousand times, she thought about leaving him then. And each time she decided to stay. Maybe it had something to do with what she thought was best for the kids. Or maybe it was because her life was otherwise pretty comfortable, inertia being so much easier than the chaos of separation. She wasn't exactly sure. Instead, she just waited for the erratic behaviour to fade away, and eventually it did.

These days, Gabe was still in good shape, and he still had all his hair. To Molly, he was as attractive now as he was when they first met. But the deep feelings evaporated years ago. In their place were a familiar fondness and an unspoken agreement that they'd stick it out together for the long haul. Their life as a couple wasn't all that bad anyway. It coasted along as a pleasant companionship most of the time, like two old friends. No more, no less.

That's why Molly decided to spend her sixty-fifth with her college gang instead of Gabe. Of course, he'd take her out to dinner either before or after her getaway. That's what one did, after all, with one's spouse on an occasion like this. But he wasn't happy when he found out she was choosing them over him for the big day itself.

"Why Willa, Molly? You haven't seen her in decades. And that Beth. She's quite the piece of work if I ever saw one."

"Do you really need to ask? They've been my friends for half a century. Hope, too. And what did Beth ever do to make you dislike her so much? You never used to feel that way."

Gabe shrugged. He knew he wasn't going to win this one. And he had no intention of explaining why he didn't like the idea of Molly spending time away with Beth. Or Hope, for that matter.

"Go ahead. Have your cozy little hen party. Forget about leaving me here on my own over the long weekend. *Really,* Molly!"

* * *

Two days after Molly's outing to *Northern de-Lights,* Gabe and she sat together in Dr. Flanagan's office. The results had come back from her magnetic resonance imaging test. Neither was prepared for what she was telling them.

"I'm afraid it's bad news, Molly. The MRI confirms it's cancer. Glioblastoma."

The doctor started to describe what was going on with the lesion in Molly's brain, but she already knew what glioblastoma was. It was one of the possible diagnoses she'd Googled when it was clear something was wrong with her. Basically, it was a death sentence.

Molly grabbed Gabe's hand and squeezed it hard. He squeezed her hand back and wrapped his other arm around her shoulders.

"How long have I got?"

"A year, more or less. Surgery might be an option. Radiation and chemo, of course. Depends on how far we take things with a treatment plan. It might give you a little more time, but– "

"Thank you, doctor. I get the picture."

As soon as they got home, Gabe convinced Molly to lie down. Then he made tea and brought it to her in her favourite English bone china cup and saucer. It was Spode, an old-fashioned rose-and-lattice pattern, long discontinued. All that remained from her mother's dinner service. He thought she might find it comforting. She did, and she was surprised when he gently covered her with a cashmere throw and lay down beside her. He wasn't usually that attentive.

"So, my girl, what are we going to do about this? Should we go for a second opinion?"

"No. I'm sure we'd just hear the same thing...I need some time to absorb this, Gabe. And I have to make up my mind whether I actually want to go through with surgery and chemo and all that. Especially if it only prolongs things a month or two. I mean, is it really worth it?"

"But Molly–"

"No, Gabe. Don't say anything. This has to be *my* decision."

"Of course. It's up to you, Molly. But I'm here for you, however you want us to handle this."

Molly turned her head to look at him. Then she cried for the first time, and there were tears in Gabe's eyes, too.

Later, over dinner, they talked about everything else but her diagnosis. How Carrie's two little ones would soon be starting a new school year in their classrooms again, no longer locked down by the pandemic. How Gabe was thinking of joining the badminton club at the recreation centre if it opened again in the fall. Even how lovely the hibiscus bush in the front garden looked that summer. Finally, Gabe cleared his throat and asked a question that had been on his mind the whole meal.

"Molly, under the circumstances, don't you think you might want to cancel your getaway with the ladies? Seems to me it might be easier on you if we have a nice, quiet birthday here at home instead."

Molly was fed up. Why does he keep harping on about this? she wondered.

"Absolutely *not*! Why cancel? It'll likely be my final chance to see them all together. And I'm not going to tell them about the cancer. I want us to have a good time. Make some great memories."

Neither of them spoke again until Gabe finished his meal and Molly started to clear the dishes.

"If this thing is going to get me, Gabe, I don't want to go quietly. I want adventures. I want fireworks. I'll have plenty of time to 'rest' after I'm gone."

Gabe didn't understand that at all. Maybe the tumour was affecting Molly's thinking again. 'Go a little wild,' she'd said. Marijuana. Fireworks. Was this how a terminally ill 65-year-old should behave?

Chapter Two

The last thing Willa Leonard wanted to do was get on a plane and fly to Ottawa, but she didn't really have much choice this time. Molly had given her plenty of notice about her birthday getaway. Six months' notice, in fact, anticipating that the pandemic would run its course in the meantime. It's hard to turn down an old friend's invitation when she sends it to you that far in advance.

Willa planned to rent a car at the Ottawa airport and make her own way to the Chateau Bord-du-Lac resort. Then she'd have to face 'the girls' for the first time in years. The four of them would be together morning, noon and night for three days. She wasn't looking forward to it at all.

She'd never been to the resort, but, according to Molly, it was a 90-minute drive from Ottawa, across the river on the Quebec side. Photos of the chateau on its website showed a grand manor built of logs and rough-hewn stone, surrounded by tall pines and white birch trees. The rustic theme carried through to the inside, with a huge four-sided fieldstone fireplace in the great hall reaching up to the rafters three stories above. There were pictures, too, of the marina and sandy beach on Lac Saint-Jacques, with guests frolicking in luminescent turquoise water that appeared suspiciously tropical. Willa was sure they were photoshopped. Lakes in Canada were never that colour. But even if it turned out that reality didn't quite match what she saw on the website, Willa had to admit it seemed idyllic. The whole place, inside and out, could easily be the setting for one of those cozy Hallmark movies. This was a trip she'd prefer not to take, but at least the destination might make up for it.

Willa had her reasons for wanting to stay away. To say they were complicated would be an understatement.

First of all, did she really have anything in common with the other three? Of course, there were the shared years at Carleton University. But that was ancient history. In the decades since then, her path and theirs had taken totally different directions.

It seemed every week Willa's Facebook news feed would fill up with the latest photos of someone's cute grandkids. Molly, Beth and Hope all had them. And then there was the all-too-frequent news of career successes: Molly's latest bestseller or Beth's record year in real estate sales. Willa's job teaching Spanish at Berlitz, the same job she'd had her whole life, just didn't seem to measure up.

And photos from Hope's luxury six-month cruise around the world with her plastic surgeon husband, taken just before the pandemic hit, had been almost too much to bear. There were dozens of them, posted every week from Bora Bora or Singapore and countless other exotic places. It was almost like Hope was trying to rub it in that her life was exciting and Willa's wasn't. At first, Willa dutifully 'Liked' each post. Then, exasperated that they clogged up her news feed, she scrolled quickly past them without looking. Finally, two months into Hope's cruise, she unfriended her.

Willa never married. She didn't have children and she never tried to climb any career ladders. Her life was safe and predictable. Exactly the way she wanted it to be. But there were times when she felt people compared her circumstances to theirs and found hers second-rate. Of course, she resented it. Who wouldn't? And that's probably what was waiting for her at the chateau, too. So why would she want to spend three days hearing about the others' exciting lives when she had nothing to brag about herself?

Things didn't used to be this way for Willa. More than the other three, she was the instigator of numerous questionable escapades in their student years. Whether it was marching on the frontlines of the protest du jour, playing strip poker with guys in the next residence, or experimenting with substances, illicit or otherwise, there wasn't much Willa wouldn't take on. When she was caught, she usually got away with whatever she wasn't supposed to be doing. Maybe it was because she had the ability to look completely innocent, as if she were every bit as surprised to find herself in the middle of dubious situations as those who discovered her there. Pale blue eyes opened wide, a pearly-white smile that accentuated her dimples, and a shrug of her shoulders were usually all it took. She projected the image of the wholesome blonde captain of some varsity cheerleading squad. But cheerleading wasn't her style, and she was anything but wholesome.

Still, there was more to Willa than parties and protests and drugs. She was fiercely loyal to her friends and close to her parents out west in Saskatchewan, especially her father Ed. She was daddy's girl, for sure. Everybody else in her extended family, and indeed in the whole small town she came from, seemed transfixed by the athletic accomplishments of Willa's older brother Dwayne, who almost, but not quite, made the Olympic biathlon team.

When she was young, Willa adored her brother too, and followed him around everywhere. That changed when she was eight and he was thirteen and way too cool to hang out with his little sister. 'Get lost' he'd tell her when she wanted to tag along with Dwayne and his friends. And he complained each time he had to babysit her when their parents went out for the evening. It happened a lot. Ed and Marion loved socializing at the local curling club, where they were regulars at 'Happy Hour' most Fridays over the fall and winter. Of course, Happy Hour was much longer than an hour. It was more like three or four. On those occasions, once their parents left, Dwayne locked himself in his bedroom and ignored Willa the entire time.

Because of this, Willa was surprised one Friday evening when Dwayne approached her with the kind of smile he hadn't given her in ages.

"Hey, sis, Mom told me to make sure you have a bath."

"I don't wanna. I already had one yesterday."

"C'mon, Willa. You're going to get me in trouble if you don't."

This seemed strange to Willa, but she reluctantly trudged to the bathroom and turned on the faucet. And when she was in the tub, she didn't like it when Dwayne said he had to check on her to make sure she was okay.

"I'm not a *baby*, you know. I can take a bath by myself!"

He slammed the door closed after she splashed him with bathwater.

Later, when she was brushing her teeth before bed, he asked her not to tell their parents what happened. This didn't make any sense to Willa. If they asked him to make sure she had a bath, why hide it? Still, she was so eager to see that smile again, she didn't say a word.

It happened other Friday evenings, too, until the time he came into the bathroom and insisted he would help her wash. First, Willa felt annoyed. Then, she started to feel super weird about the things he was doing to her. They were the kind of things her mother warned her not to let *anybody* do. He was being really, really bad, she was sure of it.

"STOP!"

Still covered in soap bubbles, Willa leaped up, climbed out of the bathtub, and ran dripping wet to her bedroom.

Dwayne called out after her.

"C'mon Willa! I was just foolin' around! I didn't mean any harm!"

Once she had her pyjamas on, she went looking for him. He was in his bedroom, with the door locked just like earlier times. She pounded on his door, but when he didn't respond, she yelled to make sure he heard her.

"I'm NEVER gonna take a bath again when Mom and Dad are out. If you try to make me, I'll tell them what you did."

For young Willa, what happened that evening just wouldn't go away. It was a naughty secret, her and Dwayne's naughty secret, and it made her stomach feel sick every time she thought about it. She had no idea that the same secret made Dwayne afraid of her, resenting the fact that she could, at any time, tell their parents on him and get him in big trouble.

Ed and Marion thought it was strange when their two children barely spoke to each other and wouldn't stay in the same room for any length of time. And they didn't like it when Dwayne refused to babysit her again, hanging out with his friends instead. It wasn't always easy making other arrangements for Happy Hour.

Later, in her teen years, Willa didn't share the enthusiasm of the others when Dwayne started to be noticed for his sports skills. How could she? She'd worshipped her big brother and he'd abused her. Made her feel dirty. And she'd had to keep it all to herself. So she focussed on her studies instead.

It turned out Willa was smart. Very smart. She skipped a year in middle school and still managed to get A's all the way through high school. After graduation, she moved a thousand miles away from home to attend Carleton University in Ottawa. And to get away from Dwayne. There were big plans for her post-graduate studies, too. She had it all figured out. She'd stay at Carleton for a Masters degree in Hispanic literature, then pursue a Ph.D. at the Universidad de Buenos Aires. Maybe she'd even wind up a professor there someday.

Then, towards the end of her senior year, those plans changed.

It was Friday, March 17th, 1978. Willa and Molly made their way along the Rideau Canal to Murphy's Pub, a student hangout not too far from campus. Molly's fiancé Gabe didn't join them that evening. He thought St. Patrick's Day celebrations were an excuse to get falling-down shitfaced. He wasn't entirely wrong. But that didn't stop Molly from going on her own with Willa anyway.

Murphy's was a traditional-style Irish pub. Not the authentic family-run kind, serving Guinness and Jameson generation after generation, but a pretty good imitation. There was dark wood paneling on its walls and ceiling and a large Smithwick's mirror hanging behind the bar. The lighting was subdued to create a cozy atmosphere, and Irish drinking songs played at low volume in the background. 'Whiskey in the Jar.' 'Black Velvet Band.' 'Wild Colonial Boy.' The regulars heard them all a thousand times. It would have been strange to hear anything else.

By the time Willa and Molly got there that evening, the place was already packed. It was the busiest night of the year. Half-plastered partiers were squeezed in together around small copper-top tables and the air was heavy, almost humid, from the warmth of their bodies. The audio system volume was cranked up to a level that risked full hearing recovery the next morning. Nobody seemed to mind, even though having a conversation was virtually impossible as a result.

The two wove their way through the crowd to seats in a far corner and settled in for an evening of green beer.

"Hey, mind if I join you?"

It was an hour and three beers later. One of the revelers at the next table decided he was more interested in staying on with them than leaving with his friends for a private party. Willa thought he was kind of cute, with wavy brown hair to his shoulders and blue eyes that crinkled in the corners when he smiled. She smiled back and he turned his chair around to face them and told them his name was Guy. They spent the next two rounds together, trying – but mostly failing – to understand what each other was saying above the noise. It didn't matter. It was easy to tell by the way he edged his chair close to

Willa and repeatedly touched her arm that Guy was more into her than Molly.

At eleven thirty, they decided to leave. Guy insisted on paying the tab for the three of them while Molly and Willa waited outside in the raw March air. He lived on campus too, so when he came out, they all took the Eastern Pathway along the canal back to the university.

Fifteen minutes later, Molly stopped at a narrow dirt trail that veered off the Pathway in the direction of Whitton House, the residence where she and Willa were roomies.

"I'm takin' the shortcut, Wills," Molly announced, using her nickname for her best friend.

Guy and Willa were holding on tight to each other as they staggered along ten feet behind her.

"We're gonna walk for a while. See you back in the room."

Molly wasn't surprised. After they'd left the pub, she'd basically been ignored by the other two. And she had no problem leaving Willa on her own with Guy. She knew that, even after so many beers, her friend could handle herself just fine.

Ten minutes later, Willa and Guy reached the Hartwell Locks straddling the canal between the campus and the Fletcher Gardens on the other side. That was when Guy closed in. There was no hesitation and no words. Just his hands grabbing at her and a sudden rough kiss.

"Hey, *stop*!"

Willa pushed him away. She wasn't about to make out with him there. It was winter, for Christ's sake. The air was too damn cold and the ground was still frozen hard. Somewhere else maybe. Somewhere warm and comfortable. But not there.

From her experience with guys, she knew they would try to see how far they could take things. Then, if she resisted, they'd back off and sulk. That's not what happened this time. Guy lunged at her again, crushing her in his arms and groping her.

"NO! I MEAN it! Jus' STOP!"

She struggled, but he didn't let go.

"C'mon Willa! I know you wanna fool around. I don't mean you any harm!"

It made her crazy, what he said. It took all her strength to free herself. She could have run away then, but instead, she pushed him so hard he lost his balance. Guy fell sideways and his head hit the cement lip of the canal wall. He didn't move after that. Willa thought she'd knocked him out. She knelt beside him and shook his shoulder.

"Hey! Guy! Get up!"

Then he moaned.

"...the *fuck*!?"

He reached up and grabbed her jacket. As he pulled her down toward him, Willa bit his hand to make him let her go and pushed back a third time. Guy rolled over the edge, almost taking her with him. The canal was dry, drained for the winter months. He hit the bottom with a heavy thud.

"Holy *shit*! Guy? . . .GUY?"

Willa peered down at him. Even though it was dark, she could still make out the shape of his motionless body. It was twisted in an awkward position on his side, arms and legs sticking out at odd angles. But his face was turned up, like he was looking straight at her. Willa was horrified. She got to her feet and stepped back from the edge so she couldn't see him anymore. Then she stood there, shaking violently, trying not to panic. What the hell should she do now? She didn't have a goddamn clue. Was there anybody else around? She looked both ways along the canal. Yes. A couple was approaching from a distance. Could they see her? Hard to tell. It wasn't a full moon that night, but almost, and there were streetlights.

She had to get away from there. Fast. She wanted to run, but all she could manage was a desperate shuffle and twice she almost tripped and fell.

When she reached the campus, Willa slowed down. After that, she wasn't sure how long she wandered around, avoiding the occasional cluster of rowdy students making their way back to their dorms, but it felt like hours and hours. In the end, the walking didn't help much. Still feeling numb, still trembling, Willa leaned against a parking lot dumpster and puked.

By the time she got to her room, it was quarter past one. It turned out she'd left Guy lying in the canal only an hour earlier. Molly was in bed but she wasn't quite asleep. Shit!

"So, you have fun with Guy?"

Willa wanted to scream. She wanted to tell Molly to leave her the fuck alone, but she couldn't. She had to act normal. Like she hadn't probably just killed someone. Willa turned her back to Molly and started undressing.

"I guess so. We walked around campus."

Willa thought she did a pretty good job of sounding calm.

"All this time?"

"Uh-huh. He dropped me off just now."

"You gonna see him again?"

Willa thought she'd explode. Why the goddamn Spanish Inquisition?

"I'm not sure." She knew her voice came out shrill this time. She couldn't help it. "I'm tired, Mo. Can we talk tomorrow?"

She climbed into bed and pretended to go to sleep, but she was awake all night.

By dawn, her brain had worked through the muddle of all those beers. After that came the hard questions. Was there any chance Guy was still alive? Sure didn't look like it. The other couple on the path, did they see her? Would they recognize her if they saw her again? And what made her freak out like that, punching him and pushing him? Why didn't she take off instead, the first time she broke free?

That was when she remembered Guy's words. They were almost the same words Dwayne used years earlier - words she never forgot - after he did those disgusting things to her in the bath.

* * *

"Jeez, Wills, you hear the news?"

"What news?"

It was late afternoon the next day. Molly had spent three hours studying at the library. She was supposed to meet Willa at the Student Union Building at five for burgers. When Willa didn't show up, Molly went looking for her. She found her back in their room, lying on the bed and staring up at the ceiling.

"Last night, they discovered a dead guy at the Hartwell locks. Looks like he fell in the canal."

"Really? That's terrible."

Willa didn't move and her voice had no emotion at all.

"You high or something, Wills? You sound spaced out."

"I'm okay. Just tired."

She was tired because of her sleepless night. And if she seemed spaced out, she was, but it wasn't because she was high. It was because she was still in shock.

The identity of the dead man was made public the following day after his next of kin were notified. His picture was on the front page of the Sunday paper and his name was Guy Sayton. Molly brought a copy of the paper to their room and showed it to Willa, who hadn't gotten out of bed all that day.

"Look at this, Wills! It's your Guy they found."

"It's too bad what happened, Mo. But he wasn't *my* Guy."

Again, the weird response, like Willa was in some kind of a trance.

"There's one thing I don't understand. It says in the article he was found by a couple around twelve thirty. But you told me he left you just before you came up to our room. That was almost *one* thirty..."

Willa suddenly sat up in her bed.

"What are you trying to say, Mo? You think I was lying? That I had something to do with it?. . .Stop! Just stop! Why make such a big fucking *deal* about this!"

The sudden flash of anger surprised them both. Willa's next words were only slightly less confrontational.

"...We were all pretty tanked, weren't we? You and me and Guy. I feel sorry for him, I really do, but who knows what happened and when? Let's just *drop* it!"

Molly didn't buy what Willa was saying. She might have been drunk, but not so drunk that she didn't remember what time it was when Willa got in. Still, she didn't push it further. She wasn't sure she wanted to know the real story.

* * *

In the last month before they graduated, it was obvious something was wrong with Willa. She seemed like a completely different person.

The confidence was gone, and her fearless pushing of limits along with it. The new Willa kept to herself. Even when Molly, Beth and Hope went to Murphy's for a final blowout at the end of exams, she wouldn't go with them.

There was a day or two when she seemed like her old self again. Molly noticed it was right after the results of the investigation into Guy's death were made public. The police concluded it was a tragic accident. He'd been partying earlier at a pub and stayed on after his friends departed. Left later on his own. Fell in the dark and broke his neck. Intoxication was a factor.

But Willa's swing back to normal didn't last long.

Molly was shocked when she learned Willa's plans had changed. She wasn't coming back to Carleton University in the fall after all. She withdrew from the post-graduate program. There would be no master's degree in Hispanic literature, no doctorate in Argentina.

Willa wasn't exactly sure what she was going to do next. She needed time to think about it, she told Molly. What she didn't mention was that, wherever her new plan might take her, it would be far from Ottawa. And she never, ever wanted to return.

Willa had no trouble choosing what to pack for the trip. She didn't have much of a wardrobe. And she couldn't begin to compete with Hope for glamour or with Beth for career-woman tailoring. Molly's style, from what Willa saw in her Facebook photos and media interviews, was more like her own anyway. It suited the image of a children's book author. Long hair, greying at the temples and pulled back into a fat bun. Little makeup, but she didn't need much anyway with her lively eyes and clear complexion. Always a colourful Indian shawl or flowing tie-dye scarf flung over something bohemian from the back of her closet. Dangly artisan earrings, and, naturally, Birkenstocks. Willa didn't have any spectacular shawls, but she matched Molly's casual look otherwise.

What she *didn't* want to take on the trip were the relentless memories of Dwayne and Guy and the two worst moments of her life. They were all jumbled up together, those moments, merged into a sad heaviness that wrapped itself around her and smothered her. These days, people called it post-traumatic stress. Willa always called it her Constant Companion. After university, it followed her out to the west coast. Vancouver was as far away as she could get from where the hurt started, and a safe - some might even say dull - life there was the only way she had been able to cope.

She was afraid that, when she saw Molly and the others again, her Constant Companion would be right there with her the whole time. But what could she do about it? It wasn't likely to leave her alone after four decades, was it?

Willa sighed as she tightened the tension straps of her suitcase, zipped it up, and rolled it to the front vestibule. Then she booked an Uber to take her to the airport.

Chapter Three

Beth Carrow was almost out the door and on her way to the chateau when her cellphone rang. It was that damn Ford couple again. She'd shown them at least a dozen houses over the past month, but they didn't like any of them. They were middle-aged diplomats returning to Ottawa from a posting in Lima and, as far as Beth was concerned, they needed to lower their expectations. Significantly.

They were calling for a second viewing of a house they'd already rejected four days earlier. And they wanted to go back *now,* at the start of the Labour Day weekend, before someone else snapped it up. It was a promising sign, even if the timing wasn't so great.

Beth contacted the vendors' agent and made an appointment for the end of the afternoon. Fortunately, the owners had already moved out, so that made scheduling easier. On the other hand, it meant she'd be late getting to the resort. She might even miss dinner that first evening. Surely Molly would understand. Showing up an hour or two late shouldn't make that much of a difference to her in the long run, should it? She'd text her after the viewing with her new ETA.

To Beth, the delayed arrival would be worth it if the Fords bought the place: her commission on the deal would be at least fifty thousand dollars. She figured she'd have more than earned it, chauffeuring the couple around to all those listings and putting up with their nit-picking about each one. And they weren't even original in their criticisms. After thirty years in the business, Beth had heard it all a thousand times.

"Totally wrong location."

Why? Because it didn't have a property developer on one side and a media magnate on the other?

"The kitchen needs a reno."

Really? The three-year-old complete makeover with quartz countertops, high-end stainless appliances, and walk-in chef's pantry not good enough for you?

"The backyard is too small."

You planning on putting in an Olympic-size pool and a tennis court too? What's the big fucking deal?!!?

Beth tried not to be cynical, but she couldn't help herself. It was a miracle she'd managed to hold back the sarcasm and hang on to her trademark Mona Lisa smile.

She was burned out. *That close* to quitting for good. And she already would have, if it weren't for the fact that the real estate market was so hot right now, with prices going sky-high since the beginning of the pandemic. Her cut, if the Fords actually purchased the property, would mean a sensational start to her retirement. Finally, she'd have the down payment for that condo on Marco Island she'd been dreaming of for ages. Or maybe, after seeing Hope's Facebook photos of twenty different versions of paradise, she might even splurge on a luxury cruise of her own. Why should Hope have all the fun?

They both appreciated the finer things, Hope and she. But there was one major difference between them: Hope relied on her husband's wealth for her cushy lifestyle, and Beth was doing it all on her own.

It wasn't that Beth had never been married. She had been, twice. Her first husband, Ben Yamamoto, was an accountant and the father of her two grown sons, Sam and David. They split up after reaching the inescapable conclusion that, having married way too young, they simply didn't like each other very much. After the divorce, he helped with child support, but that was it. She didn't want alimony or anything else from him, just a clean break.

Husband number two, Hank Butler, came along in 2001. Hank wasn't exactly Beth's idea of the perfect husband. He was a little too showboat in style and didn't always get along with her sons. But, as Molly put it, he was "Mr. Right Enough." He owned a travel agency, and Beth and he made the most of the perks that came along with it, taking multiple trips all over Europe and South America. Those trips came to an abrupt end when COVID-19 hit in March 2020. Two months later, Hank succumbed to the virus, lying all alone in the ICU of the hospital. Beth counted herself lucky she hadn't come down with it, too. She had developed asthma in her thirties and was considered particularly susceptible. After Hank passed away, she was the beneficiary of some insurance money, but any assets in the travel agency evaporated when it failed that summer. Borders had been closed. Flights had been suspended. Nobody was going anywhere anytime soon.

In the years between husbands, Beth had blossomed as a real estate agent. She kept herself busy, selling luxury houses all day long, seven days a week, and she was very good at it. Her love life wasn't nearly as successful. She was going through a prolonged dry spell in male companionship. And she was lonely.

One-night stands weren't really what she was looking for, but there were only a few and she had no regrets at all about them. What she *did* regret was a liaison of an entirely different magnitude. It wasn't just once, and it didn't happen at night. In fact, it was a full-blown affair in the fall of 1998. A series of clandestine Saturday afternoon encounters. With Gabe Bustin.

She'd always been attracted to Gabe, even as far back as university, but Molly got to him first. After graduation, there were little flirtations between them whenever the two young couples – she and Ben, Molly and Gabe – got together. It never went any further than that until after her divorce.

When it started, Beth knew exactly what brought them together. She was lonely and vulnerable, and Gabe was struggling with frustrated ambition and a successful wife who he thought couldn't possibly understand. He didn't seem to have any hesitation at all about their affair. Beth, on the other hand, felt guilty as hell. She and Molly had been friends for more than two decades at that point.

The first rendezvous set the pattern. Sam and David, still teenagers, were living with Beth, so she and Gabe had to find somewhere else. She came up with the perfect – if risky – solution. On the last Saturday in September, she would be meeting new clients for an afternoon showing in Rockcliffe Park. According to the listing sheet, the property was *"A secluded residence overlooking the Ottawa River. This home sits on a large, treed lot, with oak hardwood floors, two wood-burning fireplaces, a large master bedroom with 4pc ensuite bath . . ."*

The key words were 'secluded' and 'treed lot.' There would be no prying eyes in a neighbourhood where Beth knew more than a few people, and she liked the idea of a romantic river view. She booked time enough for two extra "showings." In her trunk, she stashed a quilt, wine glasses, and a bottle of Pinot Noir. After her clients left, she simply stayed and waited for Gabe, who was supposed to be spending yet another Saturday at the office.

For seven weekends, until mid-November, they met this way at different properties around town.

The affair ended abruptly when they both thought, but weren't exactly sure, they saw someone they recognized outside that Saturday's property. Gabe had picked her up and driven them to a semi-detached listing across the bridge from his home in the Glebe. As they left the house fifty minutes later, carelessly arm-in-arm, a black BMW approached, slowed down, and then sped up again after it passed them. Gabe immediately yanked his arm away and stepped back from Beth. The sudden movement made her lose her balance and she had to grasp the white 'FOR SALE' sign to keep from falling.

"Oh my God, Gabe. Did you see that car? Did it look familiar to you?"

"Yes . . .maybe. . . Gerrit and Hope have one like that. So do lots of other people."

"I know, but there was something about the driver. The hair. The sunglasses. She kind of looked like Hope. What if it *was* her?"

Gabe didn't answer.

Beth scurried to the passenger side door of Gabe's Subaru and climbed in as fast as she could. Gabe got in the driver's side quickly too. He started the car but left it idling. Neither of them spoke right away. They were both too upset.

"We can't do this anymore, Beth. I can't risk it."

Beth looked at him. She knew this would be coming at some point. But not now and not like this. She started crying. Then it got worse. Her chest seized up and, within seconds, it was almost impossible for her to breathe. As she gasped for air, Beth opened her purse and rifled through it looking for her puffer. Gabe, feeling helpless, looked on.

"Jesus! Can I help, Beth?"

Beth didn't answer because she couldn't. She just shook her head. When she finally found the puffer, she pulled it out, shook it hard, inserted it in her mouth, and sprayed. After she inhaled, she held her breath. Gabe held his breath too, but for a different reason. The last thing he needed was a trip to the ER with someone he was seeing on the sly.

The tightness in Beth's chest gradually went away and she started breathing easier again. For her, it wasn't the first asthma attack, just the latest of several. And it wasn't even the worst. For Gabe, it was terrifying. They didn't talk as he drove to her house. All he wanted to do was drop her off in a hurry and go straight home himself.

There were no more Saturday interludes.

In one way, Beth was relieved the fling with Gabe was over. She hated sneaking around behind Molly's back like that. Her friend deserved better. But it never stopped troubling her that Hope might have seen them.

She didn't discover the puffer was missing from her purse until several weeks later.

The unexpected viewing with the Fords meant a change in clothes. Beth left her suitcase by the front door and returned to her bedroom. In her walk-in closet, she pulled out a navy linen pant suit, her favourite white silk blouse, and patent leather Louboutins. Beth prided herself on her power dressing. It was one way of staying competitive with all the young dynamic types in her business, the ones who underestimated what this relic, old enough to be their mother, even their grandmother in a couple of cases, could do. It didn't matter that she'd won a wall-full of President's Awards in her time, to them she was only as good as her latest twelve-month sales record.

Once she finished dressing, she checked herself in the full-length mirror. She wasn't disappointed. Daily jogging kept her in good shape. Botox injections every four months smoothed out the forehead wrinkles and her precision-cropped black hair was close to her original colour before it went white. Looking pretty damn sharp for an antique, she thought, as she adjusted her designer horn-rimmed glasses, applied a fresh coat of her signature scarlet lipstick, and left for the showing.

Chapter Four

"Hello, Hope."

Gabe gave her a brief nod.

"...Gabe."

Hope didn't bother nodding back. She didn't even look at him.

That was it. A token acknowledgement of each other's presence. The last time they'd been in the same room was over twenty months earlier, at a Christmas party in 2019. There was no *'How's the old man doing these days?'* from Gabe. No *'Thanks for letting me steal Molly away for the weekend'* from Hope. Nothing like that.

What the hell ever happened between these two? Molly wondered, as Gabe picked up her suitcase and placed it in the trunk of Hope's new Mercedes. They'd never been all that friendly over the years, and today's exchange was positively frosty. It had been going on like this for far too long in Molly's view, and she'd like to patch things up between them. Now was not the time, but maybe she could have a heart-to-heart with Hope once they were settled in at the chateau. A couple of glasses of wine or even one of the joints she bought at *Northern de-*

Lights might help them relax enough to sort it out. Whatever 'it' was.

Molly made it a point to give Gabe an extra-long hug before she climbed into the passenger seat and fastened her seatbelt. He'd been sulking all morning. Telling her he already felt lonely, even before she left for the long weekend. But he'd make do, so she shouldn't worry about him being all alone while she was away having so much fun with her friends. Molly almost laughed out loud when he said that. She had no intention of worrying about him. And, after forty-odd years together, she'd seen his martyr act countless times before. Whatever the desired effect was supposed to be on her, it didn't work anymore.

Hope didn't linger. She closed the trunk of her car, got in the driver's seat, and immediately pulled away from the curb as Molly waved goodbye to Gabe.

It was the first time in a long time that Hope and Molly had been able to get together in person. They hadn't attempted another coffee date after Molly's misadventure in June. Zoom chats every couple of weeks were great for staying in touch, but talking faces hemmed in by little boxes on a laptop monitor couldn't compare to the lunches they used to have every month for years.

"I've missed you, Hope... and I must say, you're looking great. You're obviously having a good pandemic."

Hope Clift did indeed look fabulous. Fit and fresh. And young. She could easily pass for fifty. It helped that her face was the canvas for her plastic surgeon's considerable artistry, but her pretty features had exquisite symmetry even before any knife was applied the first time. Back in their university days, it was Hope who was encouraged to run for Winter Carnival Queen. She did, and she won.

She had style, too. Not everybody could carry off the diva look like Hope did. Her angled auburn blunt cut, showing no hint of her natural gray, complemented a perfect complexion kept fair by slavish year-round use of SPF 60 sunscreen. Hope wore only European designers, preferring them to North American. Their superior tailoring was a must, in her view, and she always accessorized with a flash of gold jewelry and stiletto heels. 'Better overdressed than underdressed' was Hope's fashion credo. Unlike Molly, she'd never be caught out in public in sweats.

"Thanks. I try. I have to keep looking my best."

"And how are things with Gerrit's practice these days?"

"Surprisingly good, despite COVID. But he's been thinking of retiring, and I want him to take me on another cruise."

Five minutes later, halfway across the MacDonald-Cartier Bridge to Quebec, Molly picked up Beth's text.

"Beth's running late. Last-minute showing. Says she might not be in time for dinner, so we should start without her."

"I'm not surprised. I mean, when *isn't* she working? It's a miracle she agreed to come this weekend in the first place. And who knows how long she'll stay? I hope this doesn't spoil things for you."

Am I hearing a slight edge from Hope about Beth? Molly wondered. I *really* want us all to be on good terms this weekend.

"It won't," she answered. "I'll be happy with whatever time we can have together. Let's face it, for a year and a half, we've all been locked away in our own little pandemic prisons. Now, it's like we've finally broken out, and I plan to make the most of it."

Molly looked over at Hope.

"Just getting out of the house, going to a five-star resort for my birthday with my best friends, feels like a dream to me."

Hope reached over and patted her hand.

"Good old Molly. Always the glass half full."

I *have* to be positive, thought Molly. Especially these days. If I let the cancer get to me, I'd have jumped off a bridge already.

"And when will Willa show up, do you know?"

"If her flight's on time, she should be able to join us for dinner."

"I'll be curious to see her. It's been ages. . . By the way, how's the new book coming along?"

"It's almost finished. I plan on giving it to my publisher by the end of next month. I've brought the manuscript along with me in case I have some spare time.

It needs a final edit. And it could benefit from someone else's feedback. Unfortunately, Gabe's not all that interested in my stuff these days. I think he's jealous that the books are still getting so much attention."

"Well, if you want, I'd be happy to look at it. Or maybe you can give us all a reading? And talking about readings, I've brought something we can have fun with, too. My tarot cards. I figure what better occasion than your big birthday and the end of this damn pandemic to dust them off again? The future *has* to be better than what we've been going through the past eighteen months."

"Sure, Hope. Maybe we can do it on our last night."

Molly wasn't keen on having her cards read. She already knew what the future held for her and it wasn't going to be better at all. But she didn't want to spoil Hope's mood.

They were heading east now, on Highway 50, through gaping rock cuts and over rolling forested hills. It was starting to rain.

"So how are the kids doing, Molly? Cam with anyone special these days? And Carrie's two? I bet they're growing like weeds."

"As far as I know, Cam's still on his own. He's never gotten over Wendy. I'd like to see him settle down before..."

"Before what, Molly?"

"Oh...before too much longer. He'll be forty next year, you know. It's time."

Molly paused. Hope asked about something else. What was it?

"What...what was your other question?"

"Carrie's kids. How are they?"

"They're doing great. The past year hasn't been easy, with their school closed for long stretches. But they're going back next week. And...her husband...umm...her husband..."

Jesus! Not again! Why did she keep forgetting his name? Just like at Easter. Molly was embarrassed.

"Jeremy, right?"

"Yes. Jeremy. He's been working at home all this time."

Hope glanced over at Molly with a puzzled look on her face.

"You feeling okay, girl? Maybe you should go for a rest after we check in."

"Oh, I'm fine. Just having one of my seniors' moments is all."

"*Tell* me about it. Happens to me all the time."

Hope was trying to be polite. It didn't seem to her like Molly's lapse was just a 'seniors' moment.'

After an hour, they exited Highway 50 and headed north on the road to Mont Tremblant. The resort was now thirty minutes away. Along this stretch of the route, they passed through a series of villages that, to Hope, all looked the same, one after the other after the other. Each had a couple of dozen clapboard-sided homes in various states of tidy decline lining the road, with ATVs often parked to the side. Sitting further back on larger properties were log new-builds with traditional side-gable roofs and covered front verandas. Roadside produce stands and poutine trucks hugged the village edges. Inevitably, somewhere in the centre, a sole convenience store, fronted by a DÉPANNEUR sign and sometimes a gas pump, sold everything from alcohol to home-baked goods to celebrity gossip magazines. And always, always taking pride of place was a monolithic Catholic church with a Virgin Mary statue outside, a motley collection of weather-beaten plastic flowers at her feet.

The drive was getting a little tedious for Hope. She was impatient to get to the chateau so she could relax and have a drink or two. Finally, they reached the turnoff to a winding road that led for half a mile through a nature reserve and then on to the resort grounds. A stone and log arched gateway, matching the chateau itself, signaled to visitors they were about to leave behind the drab routine of their little lives for a slice of privilege. Hope was used to luxury like this, but it was a rare treat for Molly. The second their Mercedes passed under the arch, the feeling of release it gave her was almost tangible.

Chapter Five

"Cheers, Molly! And Happy Birthday!"

"Cheers!"

Molly and Hope clinked their champagne flutes together and sipped. They had checked in an hour earlier, unpacked their bags, and come down to the lobby bar to people-watch while they waited for Willa. The guy at the grand piano beside them was playing *Bridge Over Troubled Water,* but nobody was paying any attention to him. Instead, the animated guests sitting in overstuffed sofas and chairs circling the massive fireplace were obviously in a festive mood. A buzz of exhilaration filled the place, with frequent outbursts of laughter. It was the beginning of the Labour Day weekend, the final long weekend of the summer, and the first chance for many of them to shed months of COVID-compelled sameness. Many were wearing masks, but some weren't. Molly wondered how long it would take for the rest to come off.

Perhaps it was just her imagination, but it all looked and sounded a bit forced. A brave, almost manic, show to hide the novelty of being at a resort with strangers after so many months of lockdown. The image suddenly came to her of someone standing at the open door of an airplane ten thousand feet up, poised to take their first parachute jump. That's what this feels like, she thought. Everybody's eager to make the leap but, at the same time, scared to death to go through with it. It could be a really good theme for another children's book: conquering your fears to embark on a new adventure. But would she be around long enough to see a book like that published? Not likely.

Hope took another sip and leaned closer to Molly.

"So, what's your room like?"

"It's perfect. Plenty big enough for Willa and me. And there's a great view of the lake."

Molly had booked a deluxe corner suite, the largest the chateau had on offer. While Hope and Beth could easily afford separate rooms, Molly knew this wasn't the case for Willa, so they were sharing. Besides, the two of them staying in the same suite might bring back nice memories of their time as roomies in Whitton House.

They both took another sip.

"By the way, Hope, I've been meaning to ask you how my favourite goddaughter is doing?"

Hope hesitated before answering. How much did she want to tell Molly about Audrey? She was usually guarded about the details she was willing to reveal of her daughter's life. That was because Audrey, who'd been given every advantage, every opportunity for success in whatever direction she wished to take, had lost her way.

Now thirty-eight, Audrey was Hope and Gerrit's only child. She'd inherited her mother's good looks, with thick sable hair and the kind of high cheekbones her father's patients paid thousands of dollars to achieve through surgical enhancement. But her eyes were her best feature. Dreamy. Magnificent. Mesmerizing. Audrey heard the compliments so many times they became meaningless to her. So deep brown they melted into black, and framed by lavishly arched eyebrows, those eyes won her the offer of a contract in the late nineties with a modelling agency in India. It was tempting, but Hope and Gerrit had to step in and turn it down because Audrey, at fifteen, was underage.

In high school, Audrey wasn't interested in academic achievement, and she never made top marks even though Hope and Gerrit arranged for extra tutoring. She found work at a daycare centre and continued with local modeling on the side. That was how she met her photographer husband, Arjun. The couple couldn't have been happier, especially when their son Ravi was born. That was before the car accident in 2018.

Nothing was the same after that.

It was Audrey's fault. A brief lapse in focus on the road ahead of her led to a missed red light and, a second later, a T-Bone crash into the side of a delivery van. Audrey wound up in hospital with whiplash and serious cuts to her face from flying shards of windshield glass. The ongoing neck pain was so bad, she had to take indefinite sick leave from her job at the daycare centre.

And there were no more modelling assignments. 'Such a shame, what happened to her pretty face,' was the reaction of her agency, who turned to other models on the roster instead. She was charged and later convicted for careless driving.

Molly knew about the accident, of course, and about the conviction. Hope even told her how depressed Audrey was about the scars on her forehead and around her eyes. There were repeated surgeries to try to minimize the damage, but her face would never be the same.

What Molly didn't know was that Audrey had been prescribed OxyContin to manage the whiplash pain, and that she had to take more and more of it over time to get the same relief. After three months, Arjun told Hope and Gerrit he thought Audrey was addicted. They all blamed Audrey's doctor for her slide into opioid dependency, but they suspected she was also getting more supply from less savoury sources.

Audrey and Arjun's marriage suffered under the strain. Ravi, now a teenager, was starting to act out. And then there was the time just before the pandemic when she disappeared for several days. Nobody had any idea where she went. She came back in relatively good shape but refused to talk about what happened to her while she was gone.

Now she'd done it again, taken off to God-knows-where. According to Arjun, Audrey had been missing for three days. Hope thought about pulling out of the birthday getaway, but what could she do about it? And why spoil Molly's celebration?

"She's okay, I guess. Gerrit tells me he'd like to do another touch-up sometime soon. It's not easy for her, you know. I'm not sure she'll *ever* get over the accident. Thank God she's got Arjun."

"Yes, poor thing. Thank God for that."

Hope was clearly uncomfortable talking about Audrey. She shifted her body away from Molly and started gnawing on her French-manicured thumbnail. Molly took it as a cue to change the topic. She ordered two more champagnes from the bartender and, when they arrived, asked Hope about her cruise plans.

Hope's smile returned as she described the itinerary. This time, Gerrit and she would fly to Sydney and cruise around Australia and New Zealand. There would be numerous stops along the way. Melbourne. Tasmania. Up the east coast of New Zealand to Christchurch, Wellington, Napier...

"Can I get a little bit serious for a moment, Hope?"

With Hope in full swing describing the trip, Molly figured it was a good time to try to fix things between her and Gabe. It was still just the two of them, and she might not have the opportunity after they were joined by Willa and Beth.

In her mind, Hope was cruising through the Bay of Plenty to Auckland when she was jolted back to the lobby bar by Molly's question.

"Sure?"

"Well, I couldn't help but notice that you and Gabe weren't exactly friendly when you picked me up this afternoon. It's been like that for ages now. Did something happen between you two? Anything I should know about?"

"Don't worry about it, Molly. There's nothing you need to know about."

At least that much is true, Hope thought. There was no good reason to tell Molly that she caught Gabe and Beth being a little too cozy years ago. And who knows? They might still be getting a little too cozy.

"Well, I *do* worry about it. We've been friends for decades. Surely we can talk through whatever issues might crop up..." Especially now. It was important to Molly that the people in her life be on good terms with each other. Why should there be any silly little disagreements to complicate things in the little time she had left? Life was too short – literally – for her. "...I know Gabe's not the most effusive person in the world, but he's a good man."

Really? thought Hope. A good man doesn't screw around with one of his wife's best friends, does he?

"Do we need to bring this up now, Molly?"

Molly could see Hope was getting agitated again, but she gave it one last try.

"I don't mean to upset you, Hope. I just wish we could sort things out..."

"What's to sort out? Listen, Molly...You and I are so close. Like sisters, right? That's the most important thing in the world to me. And nothing's ever going to change that."

They were nice, reassuring words, but Molly didn't answer. She wasn't getting anywhere with Hope on this. She might as well give up. For now, anyway.

It took a few seconds before they recognized Willa when she approached them. The long blonde hair was gone, but that was no surprise. Nobody their age still had the same thick hair, falling loose past their shoulders, as they did in the seventies. Willa's had faded to a weathered straw colour, shoulder-length with wispy bangs. And she'd gained weight, but that wasn't surprising either. Who hadn't put on a few pounds over the years?

The real difference was in her dull eyes and the way she held her head down and to one side, as if shielding herself from a gale. Molly vaguely recalled Willa's troubled last weeks before graduation, but she had hoped to see some trace of the vivacious rebel she had been before then. Unfortunately, there was no evidence of that spark in the muted person in front of them.

"Wills! *So* good to see you, girl! It's been *way* too long!"

Molly and Hope got to their feet and hugged her in turn. Then the three sat down again, Molly signaling to the bartender to bring them three more champagnes.

"How *are* you, and how was your flight?"

"It was okay. I'm not used to flying these days, but I guess nobody is since the pandemic hit. The flight was only half full, thank God, and we all kept our masks on. So, I suppose it could've been worse..." She looked around "...and isn't this place just *amazing*? I mean, I couldn't believe the pictures on the website, but it's even better in reality, isn't it?"

Willa heard herself talking too fast, rambling on and on to avoid any awkward gaps in their small talk. She couldn't help herself. She was as nervous as everybody else about being around other people, and then there was the extra burden of seeing old friends who might as well be strangers for all she had in common with them. She hadn't felt so uncomfortable in years. When her champagne arrived, she drained it in less than two minutes and ordered another. Willa hoped the alcohol might calm her down, and fiddling with the wine flute gave her something to do with her hands.

Molly insisted both drinks go on her tab.

It was time to return to their rooms. The dinner reservation at the resort's Chez Bella Ristorante, boasting 'Award-Winning Italian Cuisine' on its website, was for seven o'clock and they all wanted to change first. Willa followed Molly to their suite, but she wasn't looking forward to when the two of them would be alone in it together.

As it turned out, she needn't have worried. Molly relaxed on her bed, slightly tipsy after three glasses of champagne, while Willa unpacked her suitcase and hung up her clothes. There was no probing on Molly's part for deep revelations. No insinuations about Willa's strange behaviour way back when. Nothing was said that could trigger Willa's unwelcome flashbacks. Instead, the conversation was easy and light, mainly about Molly's grandchildren and her latest book, and Willa's job at Berlitz. Then, just before leaving, Molly coaxed Willa to extend her visit.

"By the way, Wills, Gabe says a special 'hi' to you. I know he'd love to see you after all these years. Do you think you might be able to stay on with us in Ottawa for a bit?"

Willa was certain Molly was just being polite. She doubted Gabe was that keen to see her. They hadn't been that friendly in university. At the time, it seemed to Willa that Gabe thought she was a bad influence on his future wife. He was probably right.

"Thanks, Mo, but I've got to be back at work by Tuesday. I only had a couple of days vacation leave left." That wasn't true. Willa had weeks and weeks of accumulated leave, but Molly wouldn't know the difference.

* * *

Chez Bella was almost full when Molly and Willa arrived, followed shortly after by Hope. The décor was typical Italian trattoria: tables covered in red-and-white checkered gingham, each lit by a single candle in a chianti bottle covered in multi-coloured wax drips. There were no plastic grape clusters framing the windows, but the folk music playing gently in the background added nicely to the ambiance.

Molly had booked the best table in the house, in a quiet corner with a view over the lake. As the three of them took their seats, Hope and she glanced at the empty fourth seat and then at each other. *Beth should damn well be here by now!* was the look Hope gave Molly, who chose not to react. Instead, she turned to smile at the maitre d' when he handed her the menu.

They selected a bottle of Prosecco but put off ordering food till Beth showed up. Half an hour later, they noticed their waiter hovering close by, pretending to straighten the napkins on the next table, but really looking for a signal they were ready to proceed.

The delay was too much for Hope. She had texted Beth right after they sat down but still didn't get an answer.

"This is crazy. I'm hungry. You ladies are too, right? Let's just start with appetizers."

Hope caught the waiter's attention and ordered mussels. Molly and Willa decided to share the antipasto. They asked for another bottle of wine. And still no Beth.

The three moved on to the main course. Lobster ravioli and chicken Fiorentina and veal gorgonzola. It was only after they finished, and their plates were removed, that Beth showed up.

"I'm *so* sorry, guys. You know how it goes. Just when you want to get away, something always pops up at the last minute that you have to deal with first...Happy

Birthday, Molly! And Willa! Long time no see! How *are* you?"

After hugging the other two, Beth barely smiled at Hope, and Hope barely smiled back. Molly noticed. Here we go again, she thought. First, the coldness between Hope and Gabe, now the same thing with Beth. What the hell is going on?

As far as Beth was concerned, there was nothing unusual in the greeting between Hope and her. It had been like that for years. Maybe Hope and Gerrit hadn't liked her Hank. Yes, he had a flashy personality. His over-the-top style didn't appeal to everybody. She was fully aware of that. On the other hand, Hope and Gerrit seemed to think they were better than just about everybody else, didn't they? They rarely socialized together in the years she and Hank were married, and when they were brought together at one event or the other, it was always the same standoffish treatment. But Hank was gone now. This was the first time she'd seen Hope since he passed, and still no warmth. Obviously, it wasn't about Hank.

That left one conclusion: Hope had something against Beth herself. And the only reason Beth could think of was that Hope did indeed see Gabe and her together. But that was over two decades ago. Beth still had her own guilty feelings about it after all these years. Did she really need Hope to make her feel even worse?

Over espressos, they discussed their plans for the weekend. Saturday's facial and massage bookings at the spa. A visit on Sunday to the artisan collective boutique in the nearby village. In between, time to relax in lounge chairs at the beach, doing absolutely nothing but drinking fancy cocktails and reminiscing. And, of course, for Molly's birthday on Sunday evening, a special dinner. They'd also squeeze in Hope's tarot card reading. The cards would reveal all, she said, and doesn't everybody want to know what the future might bring? Molly still didn't like the idea. Beth and Willa weren't exactly enthusiastic about it either. Beth figured this would turn into another one of Hope's theatrical performances, and Willa saw no reason to think her future would be any better than her past. But they hid their reactions for Molly's sake.

Molly decided not to mention the joints still tucked away in her luggage. She'd bring them out with a suitable flourish at the perfect moment. And tonight, with Hope and Beth barely speaking to each other, didn't feel like the perfect moment. Not at all.

Willa was starting to relax. She might actually enjoy herself a little bit this weekend. Maybe she shouldn't have been so worried about being with the others. They were her oldest friends, after all. Especially Molly. Of course, her path hadn't been an easy one compared to theirs. But that wasn't their fault, was it? Surely, she could feel comfortable with them. And, so far, there was no sign of her Constant Companion.

Chapter Six

"Where's Willa?" Beth asked.

She was waiting at the omelette station of the breakfast buffet. She had just selected ham and mushroom for hers and the chef was adding those ingredients to the egg mixture already bubbling in the cast iron pan. Molly, with yogurt and berries and a croissant on her plate, had wandered over to say 'good morning' before heading to the juice bar.

"She's still on Vancouver time. It's only 6 am there. She's in bed and I think she's skipping breakfast."

"Right. Of course. And Hope?"

"I don't know. She must be sleeping in, too."

Once Beth had her omelette and Molly had her cranberry juice, they sat at their table in the resort's main dining room. The tablecloths, like the servers' aprons, were crisp white linen and the silverplate cutlery was a notch up from the usual hotel-stock stainless steel. Jams and jellies waited for guests in elegant little porcelain pots, each accompanied by elegant little spoons. Scalloped butter pats in iced dishes were individual works of art, almost too perfectly formed to be smeared on the diners' bread of choice.

What a difference a day makes, Molly thought as she looked around. The hyper-skittishness about socializing during the pandemic had obviously evaporated. Facemasks were discarded even before people took their seats.

The guests at breakfast that Saturday morning looked much less fancy than their surroundings. Some wore the kind of casual attire that was de rigueur for the top one-percenters. Designer fleece and T-shirts, thousand-dollar trainers. They had perfected the image of successful forty- and fifty-something start-up entrepreneurs, some with and some without their trophy wives or their nice-looking male companions. This was the crop of business leaders who rarely bothered to grace their penthouse office suites even before the pandemic. They did all their deals on their cellphones no matter where in the world they were or what time of day it was. In fact, some were doing them now, at breakfast.

Others, like Molly and Beth, looked equally casual but less well-heeled. A retirement-age couple had come earlier and was sitting next to the windows finishing their second coffees. They'd undoubtedly worked hard all their lives to be able to afford a vacation in a place like this and they planned to make the most of it. A multi-generational family was gathered around one large round table, the grandparents finally able to enjoy post-lockdown time with their grandkids before school started again the following week. One young couple, honeymooners by the looks of them, arrived later looking sleepy and just a little bit overwhelmed by the classy surroundings.

By ten o'clock, the dining room was full, with lineups at the buffet for the maple crepes and bacon, eggs benedict and French toast. Molly and Beth had finished eating and were deliberately slow drinking their coffees. Other people might want their table, but still they lingered, waiting for Hope. It wasn't like her to be *that* late. Finally, they spotted her at the buffet, filling her plate before joining them.

"Hi, ladies. Isn't this place something else? Whenever I see smoked salmon, I can't resist."

Hope, making no excuses for showing up when she did, sat down, placed her napkin on her lap, and proceeded to eat her salmon. She kept a half-smile on her face between bites, but the way she looked told Molly and Beth something wasn't quite right. Her eyes were red and her makeup, usually flawless, looked hastily applied, with smudged mascara and lipstick on her teeth.

The truth was Hope hadn't slept in at all. In fact, she'd been awake since seven o'clock. That was when Gerrit called her with the news about Audrey.

"I've just heard from Arjun. Audrey texted him late last night. She's in Vancouver."

"She's *where*?!? What's she doing way out there?"

"Who knows? And Arjun's beside himself. Here he is, taking care of Ravi and trying to work at the same time.

Not knowing what the hell's going on with her. And she's swanning around two thousand miles away."

Gerrit was fed up with Audrey's bad behaviour. How could a daughter of his take off like that, leaving behind her husband and her son? Surely, they'd raised her better than that.

"Jesus, Gerrit! Vancouver's the worst possible place for her to be. They're dropping like flies in the streets on the East Side. That fentanyl stuff...it's an epidemic out there!"

"Don't panic just yet, Hope. We don't know she's using again. Or if she is, *what* she's using. All I know is she should get her ass back here to her family."

"Is there anything we can do to help?"

"I don't know yet, but I'll be speaking to Arjun later."

"Maybe I should come home..."

"What's the point? You'll be back on Monday anyway. I'll keep you posted."

Hope turned off her cellphone, lay on the bed, and cried. It was a nightmare, what was happening. How could she possibly enjoy the weekend when Audrey might be in big trouble half a continent away?

Eventually, Hope got up and showered. She was really, really late for breakfast. The others must be wondering where she was. Her morning routine always took at least an hour. Makeup first, then her outfit, then her hair. This time, she did it all in 30 minutes. Just before leaving her room, she inspected herself in the full-length mirror hanging inside the closet door. Not her usual polished look, but it was the best she could do under the circumstances. All part of keeping up appearances.

"Too bad Willa missed breakfast." After yet another coffee, Beth picked up her napkin and patted her mouth with it. "It was to *die* for. Will she be coming with us to the spa this afternoon?"

The three sat waiting for their bills after Hope finally finished her fruit cup. They were the last guests there and the servers were busy clearing all the other tables.

"That's the plan," Molly responded, "When I spoke to her about it, I got the impression she's never been to a spa before. But she was keen."

"Is it just me, or does she seem a bit odd?" Hope wondered. "There was something about the way she looked last evening, the way she talked. I couldn't connect with her at all. It was like she was in another world."

Beth figured she knew what was wrong with Willa.

"I remember she was like that way back when, just before we graduated. A little weird. Kind of distant. Perhaps it was all the drugs she used to do. I bet they messed up her brain. Maybe even permanently from how she's acting."

Molly didn't think it was the drugs. She thought it had something to do with that poor boy who wound up in the canal. But she didn't say anything.

Hope reacted immediately. The talk of drugs and the damage they could do was too much for her after hearing about Audrey that morning. When she felt the tears coming, she was desperate to get out of there. The last thing she wanted to do was cry in front of anybody, let alone Molly and Beth. It would simply be *too* embarrassing. And how could she possibly explain it? Hope stood up, turned to leave, and immediately collided with Willa, who had just arrived at their table. She paused only long enough to say "Sorry," and then she was gone.

Chapter Seven

Finally, it was the ideal time for Molly to bring out one of her grass cigarettes. She and the others were sitting in a semi-circle in Muskoka chairs on the beach, looking out over the lake. It was early evening, and there was nobody else nearby. The sun, its arc lower in the sky than in July, was skimming the horizon. The waning light glazed the wave tips, the sand, and the four of them with a late summer patina of burnt bronze.

They were still wrapped in terry robes from the spa, white with the chateau's burgundy logo embroidered on the chest. It was the quiet interlude between their treatments and dinner, and they were savouring the tranquil mood that lingered after hours of gentle pampering. Cocktails brought to them by a waiter, such a handsomely proportioned young man in Beth's humble opinion, added a touch of decadence.

Despite her sudden exit at brunch that morning, Hope had shown up for her hot stone massage on time and in apparent good spirits. Nobody asked, and she didn't tell, what had caused her to get so emotional. There was a brief snag in arrangements when Willa discovered her massage was going to be given by a man. For her, this was completely out of the question, and she let the receptionist and everybody else at the spa know it. She settled for a manicure and pedicure instead. Afterwards, she felt almost as mellow as the others.

Molly opened her tote bag and pulled out the joint and a book of matches.

"Well, ladies, I have a surprise for you. A little extra bliss on this perfect evening. For old times' sake." She held up the pre-rolled cigarette so they could all see what she was talking about. "I don't know about you, but I haven't smoked up in decades. And since it's legal these days, and we're all together again, I thought why not? . . . For sure they won't let us do it inside. So how about it? Right here on the beach? What do you think?"

At first, nobody answered. They were too surprised. Then Beth spoke up.

"Sure, Molly! Let's go for it!"

Hope reluctantly nodded. She wasn't totally comfortable with the idea, but she could always fake inhaling.

The others waited for Willa's response. At first, she thought about saying 'no,' but damn it, it had been forever since she'd let herself go. And she was in safe company, wasn't she? It might even be fun, as long as she didn't open her mouth and say something she couldn't take back later. Besides, she was tired of being the odd person out. She smiled and nodded too.

Molly still remembered how they used to do it. She licked the joint all over before lighting the end. Then she took a long toke to get it started, held the smoke in, and passed it to Hope sitting next to her. Hope sucked the smoke into her mouth. She didn't let it go any further, certainly not into her lungs, and after a few seconds she blew it out again. Next, it was Willa's turn, and Beth came last.

Beth inhaled deeply and held her breath. At first, there was a warm sensation in her throat, then it tickled. She wasn't surprised it felt a little bit funny. She hadn't indulged since before the boys were born. She exhaled slowly as she got up, stepped over to Molly, and returned the cigarette to her to start the sharing circle again.

The second time around, Hope changed her mind. She inhaled too.

Nobody spoke as the joint passed between them. The sound of air drawn in past pursed lips, punctuated by the occasional crackle of burning seeds, was enough.

Molly originally thought smoking grass with her old college friends would be a light-hearted diversion, and for her, that's how it was in the beginning. But there was a single sublime moment when it turned into something more. There she was, joined in a fond ritual with three women who were the closest thing to sisters she had, all of them at peace. As whisps of marijuana smoke danced away in the easy September breeze and playful waves lapped the shore in an endless gentle rhythm, Molly decided there was nowhere else she'd rather be. She was already slightly stoned. She knew that. Still, no matter what brought about this moment of complete serenity, she didn't want it to end.

The joint, almost finished, reached Beth a third time. Once more, she inhaled and held the smoke in. There it was, that weird tickling sensation again. Then the tickling turned scratchy. Invisible fingers started wrapping themselves around her chest and squeezing it. She knew what was coming.

Why did this have to happen now? *Fuck!*

Beth expelled the smoke, hoping it was a false alarm or, at least, that the asthma would calm down again by itself. It wasn't and it didn't. When the coughing started, the others thought she simply wasn't used to smoking dope anymore. She'd get over it. They even giggled. It was only when they watched her pull her inhaler out of her bag that they realized what was happening. Then they sat perfectly still while she shook it, thrust it into her mouth, and sprayed. It was several minutes, but to them it seemed like ages, before she was breathing easier again.

"Jesus! You okay now, Beth?" Willa asked.

Beth nodded. She wasn't ready to talk quite yet.

They waited a little longer. Finally, she spoke.

"Don't worry, Willa. I'll be fine. I've had it worse. This wasn't a full-blown attack, more like a warning. And I should've known better than to try to smoke *anything*...I guess I got carried away with the idea of feeling young again." Beth looked around at them all. "I'm sorry if I ruined things for you guys."

"Don't worry about that. We're just glad you're over it."

But something was bothering Molly. How come she didn't know Beth was asthmatic? She wouldn't have brought out the joint if she did.

"When did this start, Beth? I don't recall you had asthma in university."

"I didn't. The first time it happened was around the time Ben and I split up. I'm not sure if that's what brought it on, or if it was something else."

"And you didn't tell us about it?"

"I didn't tell *anybody*. I didn't want to make a big deal out of it. I'd *hate* it if people felt sorry for me. And besides, most of the time it's not that bad for me anyway. Usually only when I'm really stressed out. Or when there's a lot of smoke."

Poor Beth, Molly thought, keeping this secret all these years. And so much for my magical moment on the beach. This won't leave *any* of us with a happy memory.

Then a strange question popped into her head. A ridiculous, outrageous question, rising from one of her more unpleasant memories. It couldn't *possibly* have been Beth's inhaler she found in the car all those years ago, could it? Beth would *never* sneak around behind her back with Gabe, would she? That would be the ultimate betrayal. On both their parts.

Besides, Gabe didn't care for Beth. He didn't like it at all that Beth would be spending so much time with her this weekend...but...what if they actually *did* have an affair and it ended badly? What if *that* was the reason for the animosity?

Such an idiotic idea, Molly thought. It's the pot that's making her think that way. What were the chances there was any connection at *all* between Beth's asthma spell now and somebody's puffer left in their car more than twenty years ago?

Molly tried to shake off a vision of Gabe and Beth in bed together, but it kept coming back as she and the others left the beach and made their way to their rooms to get ready for dinner.

Chapter Eight

That evening, instead of formal dining, they chose a casual *al fresco* supper. *Al fresco* at the chateau didn't mean it was any less sumptuous. Every night over the summer months, the resort hosted a barbeque on the terrace overlooking the lake. And it wasn't just steaks, kebabs, chicken, burgers, and fish on the grills. There were separate stations for salads, seafood, pasta, cheeses, desserts, and so much more. Twenty glass-topped dining tables, each shaded by a burgundy-and-white-striped umbrella, filled up quickly with resort guests and visitors from the village and beyond who shelled out sixty bucks each to be there.

Live background music was supplied by Jean-Luc at his electric keyboard. Jean-Luc had obviously ignored the warnings about sun-induced carcinoma. His leathery skin, a dark walnut colour, looked almost elephant-hide tough. He was wearing a Hawaiian shirt unbuttoned most of the way down. It revealed a heavy gold neck chain nestled in white chest hair that didn't match the extreme black of his pompadour, a shade straight out of a home dye kit. Jean-Luc sang songs in English and French, a wide selection to appeal to the broadest audience. Engelbert Humperdinck, Cold Play, Celine Dionne, even Justin Bieber. Most of the time he managed to stay in tune, but his exaggerated vibrato, on top of his Vegas style, irritated Hope.

"Where did they find this guy?" she asked, as she returned to their table with her plate piled uncharacteristically high for the third time. Smoking up had given Hope the munchies, and, still a touch under the influence, she decided to abandon her strict diet for the rest of the weekend. "He must be a last-minute fill-in."

Beth didn't notice Jean-Luc. After recovering from her brush with asthma, she was more subdued than usual, but that didn't stop her from eye-flirting with the nice young waiter, the same one who had brought them their drinks earlier on the beach.

Molly wasn't feeling particularly friendly towards Beth, but she tried not to show it. Earlier in her suite, as she got dressed for dinner, she decided there was only one way to get past her suspicions: she would simply ask Beth straight out if she'd had an affair with Gabe. And she'd have to get it out of the way before the end of the evening, otherwise, she wouldn't be in a mood to enjoy her birthday the next day. Of course, one way or the other, Beth would deny anything happened. Molly was expecting that. Instead, it was her body language that would tell the truth. But the odds were pretty slim there'd been an affair...weren't they?

Willa speared her last shrimp, dipped it in the remaining dollop of cocktail sauce on her plate, and nibbled on the fat end. So far, the resort experience had been a revelation. The chateau was like a dream tucked away in paradise. How could she have resisted coming here? And the girls couldn't have been more friendly. Even Hope, who, contrary to her usual habit of flaunting her extravagant lifestyle, actually seemed a little bit sad. And best of all, there was no sign of her Constant Companion. It was the longest she'd ever gone without it dragging her down. That alone was cause for celebration. Willa tapped her foot to the beat of *Dancing Queen*, Jean-Luc's final offering before his break. For the first time in a long time, she was happy.

An hour later, they'd finished their coffees and were working on their second round of Baileys. Jean-Luc was packing up his gear and most of the other diners had left. Molly figured they had another fifteen minutes at most before they'd have to leave too.

"I hate to be the first one to call it a night, but I've got to check in with Gerrit." Hope drained her liqueur glass, set it down on the table, and rose to leave. She was anxious to find out if there was more news about Audrey. She hadn't heard anything from him since their early morning call.

"I'll go with you." Willa stood up too. As much as she savoured her magical day at the chateau, the togetherness had gone on long enough for her. She needed time to unwind on her own back in the suite.

"Really, you guys? We're just getting started!" Molly pretended to protest, but she wasn't disappointed that Hope and Willa were leaving. She wanted to be alone with Beth so she could get their unpleasant conversation over with.

"Guess I should go too. Big day tomorrow, right?" Beth pushed her chair back.

"Wait, Beth. I feel like a walk on the beach. Want to keep me company?"

"Okay. Just a short one, though. I need a good night's sleep after my little coughing spell."

The two got up, wound their way around the other tables on the terrace, and took the stone steps down to the lakefront. The crescent moon that evening was obscured by haze, leaving the near end of the beach in almost total darkness. A faint glow coming from the string lights of the distant marina revealed only the silhouette of a couple who passed them and climbed the stairs back up to the chateau. Then they were alone.

Molly strolled with Beth along the beach to the marina, stopping at a bench near the dock where the lights shone brightest.

"This a good place to sit for a while?"

"Sure, Molly. We can actually see each other here. It was so dark back there, I could hardly make out a thing."

Being alone with Beth, being able to watch her reactions, was exactly what Molly was aiming for. They sat on the bench and were quiet for several minutes before Molly spoke.

"We've been friends forever, haven't we, Beth?"

Beth turned to face her. Why did Molly sound so serious all of a sudden?

"Yes, of course we have. I love you to bits, girl. You know that!"

"And we've always been honest with each other, right?"

"Yes...? We have...!!?" What was Molly driving at? Beth was starting to feel vaguely uncomfortable.

"So, I want us to be honest tonight...." Molly took a deep breath before going further. "Something's bothering me, Beth. And I need you to help me understand it."

"Okay???"

"So let me start by saying that a long time ago, in the late nineties, Gabe and I went through a rough patch. Whether it was his mid-life crisis...or mine...or both...I don't know. But it was a difficult time for us."

Molly stopped and pulled a tissue out of her bag. To her surprise, she was starting to feel emotional.

"Anyway, he spent a lot of time at work back then. Even on the weekends. Or, at least, that's what he *told* me he was doing."

Oh my God! thought Beth. Is this going where I think it is? Did she find out about Gabe and me? After all this time? *Oh My God!*

"One day, I found something in our car that made me think he might be having an affair. It was on a Sunday. According to Gabe, he'd been at work the day before.

And what I found was an asthma inhaler. With red lipstick on it."

Shit! So *that's* where the damn puffer went! She remembered looking all over for it at the time. Beth frowned slightly and dug her fingernails into the palm of her hand. She was desperately trying not to show any reaction.

"I asked Gabe about it, and he said it must have belonged to a co-worker he drove home. I found it hard to believe then, and I *still* have my doubts..." Molly dabbed at her eyes and looked directly at Beth. "Today, I learned you have asthma. You had it back then, too. Beth, was it you?"

Beth didn't answer right away, but Molly could see it in her eyes. An almost imperceptible flash, gone in less than a second. Was it guilt? Pain? Embarrassment? It didn't matter. Molly knew immediately it *was* her.

Beth looked down at her lap and shook her head. She was near to tears, too.

"Oh, Molly, how could you even *ask* such a question? I feel genuinely hurt..."

Her voice faltered as she answered and there was hurt in it, but it wasn't actually a denial. Was Beth's shaky response because she regretted the affair or because, after all these years, she'd been caught?

It took Molly a while to respond. She had a decision to make. If she challenged Beth, told her she knew she was the one, it would mean an instant end to their friendship. It might even mean that the whole damn episode, dormant for so long, would lead to an ugly showdown with Gabe. And who knew where that would wind up? It was the last thing Molly wanted in the time she had left. Better to take a step back.

"I'm sorry I raised it, Beth. I should have known a friend like you would never *stab me in the back* like that."

Molly deliberately emphasized 'stab me in the back.' They were strong words. She was letting Beth off, but not lightly.

"It's okay, Molly. I understand. Like I said, I love you to bits."

Beth looked up at Molly again and tried to smile.

"We still good?"

"Yes. Of course. We're still good."

So that's how it was left. They both instantly understood the way it had to work between the two of them from then on. Beth would pretend she'd never had an affair with Gabe, and Molly would pretend she didn't know the truth. Each was pretty sure the other wasn't being honest, but as long as neither of them dropped the pretense, then it could almost, but not quite, be like it never happened. It was a fragile compromise.

They wandered back slowly across the pitch-black beach and up the steps to the chateau. Back in her room, Molly got ready for bed. And back in hers, Beth packed her suitcase.

Chapter Nine

"Wills! ...Wills! Wake *up*!"

It was just after two in the morning. Willa's moaning was loud and getting louder, finally rising to a tortured shriek. That's when Molly, ripped from her sleep by the eerie sound and not fully awake herself, turned on her bedside lamp and stumbled over to where Willa was thrashing back and forth in her twisted bedsheets.

"Wills! It's Mo. Wake up, hon, okay?" Molly kept her voice low. She tried to make the tone soothing so she wouldn't frighten Willa even more. But when Molly gently touched her arm, Willa recoiled. Then, fist closed, she punched back at whatever demon she dreamed was attacking her. Molly moved out of the way.

"*Shhhhhhhh*...Easy, Wills. It's only me. Molly. I'm not going to hurt you..."

Still half asleep, Willa sat up abruptly, her eyes opening wide in terror. But the voice she was hearing sounded familiar. Not threatening at all. When she finally recognized Molly standing beside her, she fell back on her pillows and started sobbing. Molly went to the bathroom, returned with tissues, and perched on the edge of Willa's bed.

"It's okay now, hon, it's okay. I'm here. You're going to be fine." Molly took Willa's hand.

"Oh, Mo, it was just so *awful*!"

"I can tell...But it was only a nightmare, Wills. It's over now."

"...it was about the guy at the spa. The one who was going to do my massage. He was grabbing me and I couldn't stop him..."

"No wonder you're upset...but it didn't really happen, right?"

"Right. Just a bad dream, like all the other ones."

"The other ones?"

"I've had the same damn nightmare over and over again for years. Most times, I can't see the guy's face. This time, I could."

It sounded to Molly like Willa had 'man' issues. Serious ones. But what did she know? She wasn't a psychiatrist.

"Have you tried to figure out why you keep having these nightmares?"

"I already know why." For Willa, it was obvious. The men in the dreams, whether or not she could tell who they were, were stand-ins for Dwayne and Guy. Each time, she was reliving what they wanted to do to her.

"Feel like talking about it?"

Definitely not. She'd never told another human being about either incident. Why do it now? It could only lead to trouble.

"Not really, Mo. It's hard for me to even think about it, let alone say anything."

"Well, I'm here if you change your mind."

"Thanks. I'm okay now. Sorry I woke you up."

"Don't worry about it."

Molly went back to her bed, climbed in, and turned out the light, but she couldn't sleep. What was it with Willa? she wondered. She had no problems with guys back in university. In fact, she enjoyed being with them a little *too* much. Right up until senior year. The night that boy died. What was his name again? She couldn't remember. Not surprising, since she had trouble remembering her own son-in-law's name. And after all, it happened decades ago. To Molly's knowledge, there hadn't been anyone in Willa's life in all the years since. Did that night have something to do with the way she was now?

Willa couldn't sleep either. She lay there, feeling the familiar heavy weight crushing her for the first time since she arrived at the resort. Her Constant Companion was back. She should have known it would catch up with her eventually.

"Mo?"

It was an hour later. A full hour of lying in the early morning blackness, the ugly old scenes shredding what little peace of mind Willa had left, despite her efforts to think about anything else. Years of toxic feelings swelled up inside her. Anger. Disgust. Even guilt. It *had* to come out. *Now*. She might explode if it didn't. Good thing Molly was with her. Nobody else was as close to her as Molly used to be. She'd actually been there on the worst night of Willa's life, and now here they were together again. In a way, Molly and she had come full circle.

"You still awake, Mo?"

"Yes."

"You asked if I wanted to talk about what's bothering me..."

"Yes."

"You still offering? At this ungodly hour?"

Molly could hardly hear Willa's voice, it was so faint. And she was pleading. She didn't have to.

"Of course, Wills. For you. Always."

In the dark, it was almost like the seventies all over again. That's when the two of them, lying in their dorm room beds at the end of the evening, talked about everything. Their shitload of assignments, their prima donna professors, their encounters with hot guys and losers, their worries about late periods that turned out to be false alarms. They didn't hold anything back then. Except for what Willa needed to talk about now. She was finally ready.

"It was in our final year. The time you and I went to the pub on St. Patrick's Day. You remember that evening?"

"Yes..."

"And you remember that guy we met?"

Of course Molly did. It was a big deal back then, his death. Made the front page of the newspaper. Despite her recent memory gaps, it was a tragedy she would never forget.

"How could I not, Wills? What happened to him was such a terrible thing."

"I was with him when he fell in the canal."

Willa, staring up at the ceiling, started crying again. Molly couldn't see her, but it was easy to tell from her trembling voice that Willa was still traumatized by the accident.

It *was* an accident, wasn't it?

"Go on...?"

Then it all poured out of her. Guy's attack and how she stopped him. How she could have – should have – run away from him then, but didn't. She fought back instead. And how, in the end, he died because of it.

By the time Willa finished telling her story, Molly had turned the light back on and returned to her bedside.

"I feel *so* sorry for you, Wills. Living with this for so long. But can I tell you something? Nothing you've just said surprises me."

"Really???"

"Yes, really. At the time, I figured you might have been with him when it happened. There was something about the way you were acting when you came back to our room that night..." And how she'd lived her life ever since. But Molly kept that thought to herself. "...How come you didn't report it, Wills?"

"I was afraid they'd blame me for his death. That I'd get in deep shit. Thrown in jail or something. So I kept it to myself. I always have."

"You said you pushed him away in self defence, right? And his fall was an accident?"

"Yes...absolutely! You believe me, don't you?"

"Of course I believe you, Wills. Still, there's one thing that puzzles me. You said you could have broken free away at one point. Why didn't you?"

"Because...because..." Willa hesitated. But now that she'd told Molly one part of her story, she might as well tell her the rest. "...because what he did...what he said...was almost exactly like something Dwayne said and did to me when I was a kid. And I lost it. I couldn't stop myself. But I certainly didn't mean for him to die."

Willa's brother! He molested her?!? Molly knew Willa wasn't close to him, but she'd never mentioned *that* before.

"Jesus, Wills! And you've carried that around all these years, too? What Dwayne did to you?"

Willa nodded.

"I *adored* Dwayne. He was my hero. And then he ruined *everything*..." She stopped to wipe her tears with an already-soggy tissue, then grabbed another. "...The sick things he did, they were always there in the back of my mind. And that night...when Guy attacked me...and said almost the same words as Dwayne...well...I just went crazy..."

Molly wrapped her arms around Willa and they stayed that way, not speaking, until Willa's crying stopped and her breathing was normal again.

"Can I tell you what I think, Wills?"

"Sure. Go ahead. But please don't tell me you hate me. I couldn't *stand* it if you said you hate me..."

"Hate you? Of course not. I feel bad for you, hon....and I think you need help dealing with all this. I'm no expert, but I'm pretty sure you have PTSD. Maybe you already know that. Have you ever thought of going for therapy?"

"Yes. Countless times. But it would mean I'd have to talk about this with another person. I could never bring myself to do that...until just now, with you. And I was always scared the therapist might go to the authorities."

"I'm not sure a therapist would actually pass along anything a patient told him or her in confidence. Not unless somebody was in danger. Which isn't the case with you."

For the first time, Willa thought someone else knew her whole story, all the unspeakable details. She'd left nothing out. It was the right thing to do, telling Molly. That's how it felt at that moment, anyway. She might regret it in the morning, but now there was only relief.

And now Willa felt more exhausted than she'd ever been before.

"Thanks for listening, Mo. It's been hell on earth living with this for such a long time. And I'll think about a therapist. I promise. Right this second, though, I'm so tired I could sleep for a week." And this time, she hoped, there won't be any nightmares.

Molly squeezed Willa's hand, then returned to her own bed.

"Me too...Love you, Wills."

"Love you, Mo. And by the way, I guess I can now officially say 'Happy Birthday!'"

Sure, thought Molly. My birthday. I hope I can be awake for at least some of it. Then she curled up in her favourite position on her side, pillows arranged just so, and drifted off.

Chapter Ten

Oh shit! Hope. Alone. Why couldn't it be like yesterday? Beth wondered. Yesterday, it was just Molly with her at breakfast, at least at the beginning. The last thing Beth needed right now was to sit across the table from someone who'd barely spoken to her over the years. It would be way less awkward if Molly or Willa were there to keep the conversation going.

Beth lingered beside the bread selection near one end of the buffet table where Hope couldn't see her. Should she sneak out while she had the chance? That would mean leaving the chateau without eating, and what a drag *that* would be. Beth was famished, and the food looked *so* good. Not to mention she'd paid for the room-plus-breakfast-buffet package.

The sweet fragrance of warm Danishes in the large basket next to her seduced her into staying, but only long enough for the meal. After the conversation with Molly at the marina the night before, Beth didn't feel comfortable about being there even one minute more than that. She was ashamed about the affair, of course. And she was pretty sure Molly saw through her denial, even though she said otherwise. But it would likely confirm Molly's suspicions if she didn't see her before she left. Eating breakfast together and giving her a birthday gift was the least she could do. Then she'd go.

Beth spent extra time at the buffet, waiting for the others to show up so she wouldn't have to sit on her own with Hope. One Danish, a slice of ham, and a generous helping of scrambled eggs later, she gave up.

"Good morning, Hope."

"Good morning, Beth. You look particularly corporate this morning. Almost like you're about to present the latest sales figures to head office."

This wasn't intended to be a compliment, and Beth knew it. But it was true. She'd packed all her casual resort gear in her suitcase and left it with the concierge. Instead, she wore the same navy linen suit she arrived in, the same Louboutin shoes. She had decided to give a work excuse for leaving early and wanted to look the part.

"I had a call an hour ago from a client."

It was a lie. Beth had a lot of practice at lying. This one, she figured, would do the trick nicely.

"I've got to head back to Ottawa. Really bad timing, I know, but that's the way it goes in my world."

Hope, looking skeptical, popped a melon ball in her mouth and spoke around it. "On a Sunday morning? And Molly's birthday as well? What a shame! She'll be *so* disappointed. I know she's been counting on *all* of us to be with her the whole weekend, and especially today."

Go ahead, Beth thought. Rub it in. Last night's talk with Molly already made her feel bad enough. Why not pile on her early departure, too?

"Real estate agents don't keep regular hours, you know. And *some* of us still have to make a living. I'm sure she'll understand."

"Maybe. Maybe not."

Beth shrugged and gave up. They ate in silence for the next eight minutes until Molly and Willa arrived together from the buffet and placed their full plates on the table.

"HAPPY BIRTHDAY, MOLLY!"

Hope leaped up and gave Molly a hug with a flourish that got the attention of diners at the surrounding tables. How typical, Willa thought. Beth also hugged her, but her greeting was more muted.

Over final coffees, as their server presented the bills, Beth made her excuses.

"I'm *so* sorry, Molly, but I've got to get back to the city. I had a call this morning from that annoying Ford couple I told you about. They want to make an offer on the house I showed them on Friday."

"I was *wondering* why you were dressed to kill!"

Molly had a mixed reaction to Beth's early departure. Was catering to difficult clients more important to her than a close friend's special birthday celebration? The obvious answer was 'yes.' But she had a sense that something else was driving it, too. Most likely, this was more about the uncomfortable conversation they'd had the evening before, and Beth's less-than-convincing denial. Molly, herself, was having trouble with the situation. Maybe Beth's leaving now was a good thing for them both.

Beth pulled a birthday card out of her bag and gave it to Molly.

"But before I go...for you, Molly..." She reached in again and brought out a small box wrapped in sparkly mauve tissue paper. A sprig of artificial lavender was captured in the bow of its purple corkscrew ribbons. "...love you so much, girl!"

"You really didn't have to, you know..." The protest was a formality. Molly opened the card first, then unwrapped the present. She put on a smile when she saw the earrings, silver hoops with a row of tiny rubies following the curve of each.

"Oh, Beth, you shouldn't have! But thank you. Thank you so much! They're *gorgeous*!" Again, proper words of gratitude, slightly less enthusiastic than if the trust between them hadn't been broken. Molly squeezed Beth's hand and proceeded to put the earrings on to be admired by the others.

"Well, I must be off." Beth stood up to leave. "Bye, ladies. So good to see you all. And Willa, don't make it so long before your next visit." She leaned over to give Willa a kiss on her cheek. Then, when she reached the arched entrance to the dining room, she turned, waved a last time, and disappeared.

Hope returned to her room after breakfast and was getting ready for their outing to the village when Gerrit called.

"Damn it, Hope. We gave that girl everything. The best schools. Travel. A car. Everything. And what thanks do we get? She turns herself into a drug addict. Abandons her husband and child. *Our grandchild.* Almost winds up dead. What the *hell* is she thinking?"

Hope was already crying, and Gerrit's rant just made it worse.

"Please don't go on like that, Gerrit. I can't handle it."

They'd spoken the previous evening, too, but there was no news about Audrey then. This morning, there was. And it wasn't good. Audrey was still in Vancouver. The previous day, she'd overdosed in a cheap hotel in the Downtown East Side. Cleaning staff found her unconscious, and an ambulance took her to hospital where, fortunately, she recovered. Arjun had just dropped Ravi off with Gerrit and was heading out to the airport for the next flight west.

"Do you think she'll come back with him, Gerrit?"

"If she knows what's good for her, she will. But he's got to get to her first, before something even worse happens."

"Do you need help with Ravi? Should I come home?"

Hope didn't want to be the second friend to abandon Molly on her birthday. She had to offer anyway. Family was more important.

"No, I'm good for now. And anyway, I'll see you tomorrow."

* * *

The phone also rang back in Molly's suite.

"Happy Birthday, Molly!"

"Thanks, Gabe."

"How are you feeling? No headaches, I hope. No dizzy spells?"

"No, thank God. Fingers crossed I won't have any of that misery today."

"And you're enjoying your time with the girls?"

"Well, we all had a wonderful afternoon at the spa yesterday...but there's only three of us now. Beth left this morning. She took off an hour ago."

"Really? Why? Did something happen?"

Gabe sounded a little too concerned about Beth's early departure. Was he worried that, at one wine-soaked moment or the other, there might have been a slip-up by Beth about their little liaison? Molly decided she wasn't going to make it easy for him.

"She went back to Ottawa for work. Some clients want to make an offer on a property. But I think it was more than that. It was like she could hardly wait to get away. I wonder why?"

"Well...I wouldn't try to dig too deep if I were you. Who knows what she might come up with?"

"Oh? You know something I don't? You think she might have another reason to take off early on my birthday?"

Molly could imagine Gabe squirming at the other end of the phone.

"I simply wouldn't trust her. That's all I meant to say."

"Hmmm... I'm not sure where you get that, Gabe. But anyway, enough about Beth."

Gabe was more than willing to change the topic.

"So, what are your plans for the rest of the day, Molly? Doing something special, I expect."

In an instant, his tone changed from guarded anxiety to righteous resentment. His feelings were clear. It was *so* unjust for her to treat him like that, leaving him behind while she took off with her so-called friends to have fun on her birthday.

"We're going into the village to do some shopping and have a late lunch. I think the girls have planned something for my birthday dinner, and then Hope wants to read our tarot cards. I'm not so keen on that part. But, yes, it will be special."

"Well, good for you." This time, it was undisguised sarcasm.

Oh, grow up! Molly was tempted to say. Instead, she decided to smooth things over.

"Gabe, how about we go out for a nice quiet supper after I get back? We can have our own little celebration. I would really like that...wouldn't you?"

"Sure, Molly."

He sounded only slightly consoled, but it was the best Molly could do. Or wanted to do.

"Great, then. Got to dash, Gabe. Willa and Hope are already down in the lobby, wondering where I am."

"Of course. Can't keep your friends waiting, can you?"

What a lame conversation, Molly thought, as she tucked the key card in her purse and left her room. Sometimes Gabe could be such a jerk.

Chapter Eleven

The weather was spectacularly hot and humid for that time of year. The air, heavy with the voluptuous scent of a thousand blossoms, conjured up a Caribbean paradise rather than pastoral Quebec. Under the hazy blue sky, on either side of the chateau entrance, lush botanical beds bursting with black-eyed susans, pink cosmos, purple coneflowers, and orange hibiscus defied guests to pass by without admiring the unruly palette. Just beyond the manicured lawns, the nature reserve enticed visitors to explore its hidden places under the shade of the wild forest canopy. The call of cicadas from the trees was a fitting soundtrack for the tropical ambiance that day.

Molly, Willa and Hope soaked up the flamboyant display of late summer colours as they watched for the shuttle that would take them to the village. According to the uniformed doorman, red-faced and visibly wilted in the heat, a thunderstorm was forecast that afternoon. There was no sign of it now. Hope took the large umbrella he offered just the same.

Today is simply perfect, Molly thought. She needed more days like this. Too many of her precious hours were spent cooped up inside her house writing stories, and when she did have time to explore her neighbourhood, the urban version of outdoors just couldn't compare. Instead, it was all boxy front yards and tidy back decks with civilized patches of grass beyond. The nearby park, ruthlessly mowed and deliberately bereft of overgrown green spots that could conceal questionable transactions, appealed mainly to early-morning joggers, people with little kids and dogs, and older folks who needed easy terrain.

The shuttle pulled up, but Molly decided not to take it. She could get on a bus any old day.

"You guys go ahead. I'm going on foot," she said as Willa climbed on board and disappeared inside.

Hope stopped and turned around on the shuttle step.

"But Molly..."

"No. I mean it." Molly swept her arm toward the nature reserve. "I want to enjoy all this. I may never have the chance again."

"Of course you will. Gabe would bring you here in a second if you asked him."

Molly knew *that* wasn't going to happen. Too little time left to her, too little inclination on Gabe's part to splurge on a place like this. She'd never be coming back.

"Maybe. But it's such a magnificent day, I think I'll walk through the reserve. I read somewhere it takes less than half an hour to get to the village that way. I can meet you at the restaurant."

"You sure, Molly? Want some company?"

It was a nice offer. Molly knew Hope would rather take the bus.

"Thanks, but no. Enjoy the ride, you two. And when you get there, order me a glass of white wine, okay? I won't be long."

"Okay." Hope didn't want to leave her on her own, but what else could she do? Molly's mind was clearly made up. "See you soon."

Hope climbed the last step, the door closed behind her, and they drove away.

* * *

An unexpected little adventure in the wilderness. What a treat! And *so* liberating. Molly hummed *Three Little Birds* as she strolled along the resort's main road towards the trail that led off it into the reserve. When she was sure nobody else was around, she started singing low. *'Don't worry 'bout a thing, cause every little thing is gonna be alright...'* Just then, everything felt perfectly alright to Molly.

The trail she chose wasn't the only entry to the woodlands. There were several, with crisscrossing paths off each that led to different features. The reserve was open to the public all year round. In the winter months, it was well-travelled by dog sledders, cross-country skiers, even Christmas partiers in horse-drawn sleighs. Today, it wasn't busy at all. The only people Molly encountered were a middle-aged couple who emerged from the trees as she started her walk, and a jogger further along whose breathless "Hi!" was punctuated with droplets of sweat as he breezed past her. Otherwise, she was on her own. She was okay with that. In fact, she preferred it. And she wasn't afraid of getting lost. There were signposts everywhere.

Molly paused when she reached one at the intersection of two paths where a weathered wooden arrow, carved with the word "Chapel," pointed left. A chapel...hidden away in the woods... it sounded like something from a fairy tale or a cozy mystery novel. It wasn't on the direct route to the village, but surely she could take a little extra time to visit it. Sit in the quiet for a bit and meditate. This day, of all days, she deserved a few calming minutes with herself, didn't she? Hope and Willa wouldn't mind if she were just a tiny bit late. She was confident they would allow her this self-indulgence on her birthday.

Molly padded down a gentle hill on the winding secondary trail, her footsteps silenced by a carpet of fallen orange pine needles. Most of the way, the glare of the sun was held back by the trees, but every so often, rays of light poked through, dappling the path itself and the moss and dry leaves bordering it. The further she descended, the cooler, the more refreshing, the air felt.

Finally, after crossing an old footbridge over a dry stream bed, she reached the chapel. It was the kind of sanctuary, picturesque and romantic, that might be featured in a "Hidden Gems of Quebec" calendar or serve as the ideal setting for somebody's wedding. It would have to be a small wedding, though. From the outside, it looked like it could hold a dozen people at most. It had old stone walls and a miniature bell tower. Its heavy oak door was gothic in style, with a pointed arch and wrought iron hinges and handle. And it was locked.

Well, *that's* a disappointment, Molly thought. So much for stealing a few precious moments of peaceful reflection inside. She went to a window and tried to see in, without success. There was only blackness.

Even though she couldn't enter the chapel, she could still take a few minutes to savour the quiet of the glen before climbing back up to the main trail and resuming her walk to the village. Molly looked around for a place to sit. A gap between the roots of a spruce tree a few yards away looked just about right. Molly settled cross-legged at its base, letting her head fall back against the trunk.

* * *

"Two glasses of Sauvignon Blanc and a Perrier, please."

Sitting on the front patio of the village bistro, Hope and Willa agreed to hold off ordering their meals until Molly showed up. It was a busy spot. Every table was taken, and more people were lined up at the hostess station in front. As far as they could tell, pizza from the in-house wood-fired oven was the most popular menu item, both with the customers and with the wasps that kept buzzing around their food even though they were repeatedly swatted away. On the other side of the road was "Les Cinq Canards," the artisan gift shop they planned to visit after. Its sidewalk display table was cluttered with a jumble of dipped beeswax candles and fancy mustards, pottery mugs and rough-cut squares of scented soaps. None of it was Hope's style, but Willa had her eye on a handwoven wool tunic that hung next to the gingerbread-trim screen door. And perhaps she could find something inside as a birthday gift for Molly.

"We haven't had much of a chance to chat this trip, have we, Willa?"

No, Willa thought, they haven't. But that was okay. She really didn't need to hear any more about Hope's pampered life. Still, she wanted to keep the small talk going until Molly showed up. Anything to avoid an awkward gap in the conversation.

"You're absolutely right. So, let's catch up now. Tell me, how is Gerrit doing?"

To Willa, everything Hope said about Gerrit's thriving business and their next cruise was totally predictable.

"And Audrey's little family?"

Hope's expression changed instantly, from cheerful to wounded, almost like the question had slapped her in the face. Her chin trembled and tears started to fill her eyes. Willa had never seen her like this before.

"You okay, Hope? Is something wrong?"

Hope shook her head to deny it, even though the tears now trickled down her cheeks. She couldn't help it. She grabbed her napkin off the table and dabbed at the wet spots, then gave Willa an embarrassed grin.

"I'm sorry, Willa. You must think I'm a basket case...and so must everyone else."

Hope looked around at nearby tables to see if anybody else noticed, but the other diners were too busy eating and drinking and talking to each other.

"Don't worry about it. Who cares what other people think anyway?"

But Willa knew Hope *did* care. Good thing nobody was paying any attention to her now.

"...It's just that I...I got bad news about Audrey this morning and I'm having trouble dealing with it."

Willa didn't ask about the bad news. She didn't want to pry. Hope would talk about it if she wanted to. It turned out she did.

"If I tell you...promise me you won't mention it to the others?"

"Of course not." Willa had her own sad secrets, shared the night before with Molly. She had no intention of passing along Hope's, no matter what it was.

"You remember Audrey had a bad car accident a while ago?"

"Yes..."

"Well, she was on painkillers for a while because of her injuries. Oxycontin. And she developed an addiction to it. I blame the doctor who kept prescribing it to her, cranking up the dosage. I mean, what the *hell* was he thinking?!?"

Hope stopped as the server approached their table with the drinks. As soon as he placed them on the table and left, she carried on.

"Anyway, it's been a total nightmare for Gerrit and me and Arjun. For a while, she recovered, and things were looking good again. But now she's relapsed. And even worse, she went missing earlier this week. At first, we had no idea where she was. Now we know."

"Oh my *God*! I hope she's okay?"

"No, she's not. Gerrit tells me she's in Vancouver. Found unconscious yesterday afternoon in some sleazy hotel. Thank heavens, they got to her in time and sent her to the hospital. She was discharged last evening. Arjun is flying out today to find her and bring her back...oh Willa, I feel so *helpless*."

Hope started crying again. It was full-blown sobbing now, only partly smothered by the already-damp napkin she held up to her face. The people at the next table finally noticed. When they turned to stare, Willa was tempted to speak up, to tell them to mind their own business. Instead, she shook her head and gave them a dirty look. They got the message and went back to their beers and pizzas.

"Is there anything I can do, Hope? I'll be back home tomorrow evening. Arjun can call me if he needs help getting around Vancouver."

This feels strange, thought Willa. Here she was, offering to help Hope, the last person on earth she thought would ever need it. Her perfect life wasn't so perfect after all. Why did she ever assume Hope never had to face real-life problems? Even big money can't insulate you from that.

It took several minutes for Hope to calm down enough to answer. She steadied her breathing, placed the bunched-up napkin on the table, and smoothed back her hair. She felt totally mortified. All she wanted to do now was leave and have lunch somewhere else. Anywhere else.

"Thanks, Willa. You're a sweetheart! I'll let him know...but can we find another place to eat? What about the pub we passed a block back? If it's okay with you, I'll call Molly and suggest she meet us there instead."

Willa looked at her watch. Molly should have shown up by now. In fact, she was a few minutes late.

"Sure. Go ahead, call her. I'll ask for the bill."

Willa caught the waiter's attention while Hope speed-dialed Molly. But the call didn't go through. She tried a couple more times.

"That's strange...it keeps going straight to voice messaging. I'll keep trying. But let's leave anyway. We can pop across the street and do some shopping while we keep an eye out for her."

***

It was the low rumble of thunder that woke Molly up. How long had she been sleeping? She pulled out her cell phone. Forty minutes. Oh, *shit*! Willa and Hope must be worried about her. She'd text them, let them know she was okay. Then she'd get to the village as fast as she could. But her phone couldn't find a connection. She stood up and raised it over her head. Maybe holding the damn thing up high would do the trick. It didn't.

Molly scrambled up the gentle slope in the same direction as she came. At least, she *thought* it was the same direction. But wasn't there a footbridge somewhere on the way? Where did it go? And where exactly *was* she?

Ten minutes later, she wound up back at the chapel, confused and dizzy. Not again, she repeated to herself over and over. Don't let this be happening to me *again*.

More thunder. And now, drops of rain, too. Not a lot, but enough to make her feel even more miserable.

Maybe she should stay put. That's what they say is the right thing to do when someone is lost in the wilderness. Sooner or later, somebody would come looking for her. She just hoped they could hear each other over the noise of the approaching storm.

"Jesus, Molly! Are you okay? What happened to you?"

Molly leaped to her feet as Hope rushed over to her and held the resort umbrella over her head.

"Thank *God* you found me! You have no idea how glad I am to see you. I got lost and I'm soaking wet and I was beginning to think I'd be stuck here forever."

After spending half an hour at the artisan shop waiting for Molly to show up, Hope and Willa knew something was wrong. They decided to go looking for her in the reserve. Michel, the son of one of the shop owners, volunteered to be their guide. He knew the trails well and was more than happy to get out of his shift at the cash register.

"Of *course,* we found you. We wouldn't stop searching until we did. Can't leave the birthday girl alone in the woods, can we? Let's get back to the resort. It doesn't look like this crappy weather will let up any time soon."

Michel escorted them up the path and over the footbridge to the main trail. He pointed out the right direction to the resort before heading back in the opposite direction to the village. Once he was out of sight, Molly was all apologies.

"Damn dizzy spells. And losing my way like that! I don't know what's gotten into me lately. Getting old and decrepit, I guess. I'm so sorry I caused you all this trouble, guys."

Of course, she knew exactly what her problem was, and it was a whole lot more than getting old. But telling her friends about the cancer now would just make things worse.

Hope and Willa looked at each other. Molly's behaviour screamed out something much more serious than simply old age. What on earth is going on with her? Hope wondered. First, the memory lapses on the way to the resort. Now this. How could she get lost when the trails were so well marked? All she needed to do was follow one of them till she reached a signpost.

"Don't worry about it, Mo," Willa said. "We're just glad we found you when we did. Someday you'll have a good laugh about all this."

"I doubt it," Molly said.

"And don't you think you should see a doctor about these spells?" Hope asked.

Already did that, Molly thought.

"Good idea," she replied.

Chapter Twelve

"Make a wish, birthday girl!"

The elegant cake in front of Molly had teal ombre fondant icing embellished with clusters of pastel buttercream flowers, lit up by half a dozen gold glitter candles. Molly closed her eyes and tried to think of something to wish for. Something that wasn't totally impossible, like her brain being somehow magically healed. She knew *that* wasn't going to happen, so why waste a perfectly good wish on it? Instead, she thought of the next best thing: a peaceful passing with family by her side and no pain. Didn't everybody want to go that way? Molly pictured the scene in her mind: she was comfortably tucked under her grandmother's heirloom patchwork quilt in her own soft bed, gradually drifting off, gentle and easy, to whatever celestial existence might be waiting for her. It actually made her smile. Molly opened her eyes, took a deep breath in, and blew on the candles. There was no need for a second try. They all went out the first time. Molly wasn't superstitious, but she chose to take it as a sign her wish would come true.

The three of them were sitting at a small table in Molly's and Willa's suite. Off to one side was a waiter's cart, where Willa had moved the remains of their dinner, now hidden under used linen napkins and stainless-steel plate covers. Originally, Hope had planned to hold the birthday dinner in one of the chateau's private dining rooms. She'd booked it months ago. But after Molly's misadventure that afternoon, they decided room service would be better.

"We can keep it cozy," Hope said. "Just us on our own."

Molly didn't protest. After they'd returned to the chateau, she immediately went to the suite to rest. She was surprised when she woke up, still exhausted, a full two hours later. A fancy dining room meal, and all the fuss that went with it, wasn't so appealing anymore.

The mood in the suite was laid-back, the food simple. They didn't compromise on the champagne, but nobody wanted haute cuisine that evening. No filets mignons and heavy sauces, no truffle risotto or sautéed kale or any other pretentious offering. Instead, it was burgers and fries. They were gourmet burgers, of course, and fries sprinkled with pink Himalayan salt flakes, but burgers and fries just the same.

Molly was determined that Gabe would never know about the change to a low-key celebration, and especially not what had happened to her that afternoon. It would give him too much satisfaction to learn he was right all along about her having a quiet birthday. If he ever found out, he'd crow about it for sure. "I told you so," he'd say. How many times had Molly heard *that* before? And she wouldn't put it past him this time either. She'd rather gloss it over or make it sound more exciting instead. After all, she was a pretty good storyteller, wasn't she?

Willa was the first to finish her piece of cake, then she went to the closet. She brought out a gift bag that she'd stashed there earlier and presented it to Molly.

"I have a little something for you, Mo. Hope you like it."

Hidden inside, under lime green tissue paper, was a batik scarf. Rose and indigo, Molly's favourite colours.

"Oh, Wills, I *love* it," Molly immediately draped it around her neck. "It's *perfect*! Thank you so much!"

"I'm glad. When I saw it in the Cinq Canards shop today, I thought 'this looks just like Molly.'"

It was Hope's turn. Instead of her usual ornately wrapped present, she opened her Vachetta leather handbag, fished out an envelope, and handed it to Molly.

"Happy Birthday, Molly. This is something we can enjoy together..."

Molly opened the envelope, took out the card, and read it. A trip for two the following summer to Prince Edward County. Her first thought was not a happy one and she frowned. Bad manners, she realized, and quickly corrected it with a forced smile.

"What a lovely idea, Hope. Thanks so much."

Hope didn't pick up on Molly's mixed reaction.

"I've always wanted to visit there, you know." Hope was already excited. "I'd love to take one of the vineyard tours, maybe even a couple. And check out the antique shops. I hear you can get some good bargains there. So I thought, why put it off any longer, right?"

Hope nodded at Molly, and looked for Molly to nod back. She didn't.

"...Gerrit isn't interested in going. 'A sissy trip,' he called it when I asked him...And anyway, who better to enjoy it with than you, Molly? We'll have a fabulous time. I've already booked a five-star B-and-B for next June, but I can change the dates if that doesn't suit you. Gives us lots of time to plan for it, right? . . .What do you think?"

What did Molly think? She knew exactly what she thought. To her, it was crystal clear. The odds were against her being around next June. And, even if she made it to then, she wouldn't be in any shape to go anywhere, let alone take winery tours or shop for antiques. But now was not the time to explain this to Hope.

"Sounds wonderful, Hope. And June would be such a nice month for it..." Molly tried to sound convincing, but it didn't quite work for her. She could hear the weariness in her own voice. It didn't seem to register at all with Hope.

"Great! I can hardly wait."

Half an hour later, they were still sitting around the table sipping Grand Marniers when Hope brought out her tarot cards.

"Think of a question, Molly, but keep it to yourself for now."

Molly nodded. She really didn't want to play along with this, but what choice did she have? Hope had been reading their cards for years. She would think it was strange if Molly balked now, especially since it was her birthday.

So, what *should* she ask? It was obvious. There was only one thing weighing on her mind. Morning, noon and night, even when she tried to push it away, it was always there: the cancer diagnosis. Nothing else was half as important. She didn't have any hope at all of beating it, but what might the cards say?

"You know how it works. Go ahead and shuffle the deck while you think about your question."

They'd done this so many times over the years, Molly was used to the routine. After shuffling, she cut the cards, placing them face down in three piles. Then she put the three piles back together again in random order and passed them to Hope. Hope turned the shuffled deck around and laid the top six cards face up in a simple Celtic Cross spread. One card for the essence of the matter. The second for the present. The next for the near future. The fourth representing Molly in that future. The fifth was the best she could hope for. And finally, the ultimate outcome.

"Now you can tell me your question, Molly."

"I want to know...what will be happening with my health over the coming year?" Molly didn't say more. She didn't want to influence Hope in her reading.

Hope thought the question was strangely worded. There seemed to be an expectation Molly's health would somehow change. But Hope wasn't entirely surprised this was the focus. She'd been worried about Molly's mental lapses ever since their drive to the resort, especially given what happened that afternoon in the forest. Molly must be worried too.

She sat quietly as she studied each card, both on its own and in combination with others spread out on the table. No matter how she tried to interpret them, it didn't look good. In fact, she'd rarely been confronted with a more challenging reading. Hope kept a rigid smile on her face as she sorted out what the cards told her, and what she wanted to say to Molly. They were two different things entirely.

The seven of pentacles was the first card in the spread, the crux of the issue. A bad place to start. It indicated serious health problems causing Molly anxiety.

The six of cups came next, for the present situation. The card had elements of a celebration. That's right, Hope thought. We're all here for Molly's birthday. But it could also signify exhaustion. Molly must feel her body was out of sorts due to her health problems.

For the near future, the ten of wands. Whatever illness Molly may have, it will be made worse by worries and overexertion, with no immediate relief in sight.

According to the four of swords, Molly, herself, in the future will have to rest and try to recuperate, but her problems will not go away. She will need further medical attention.

The best outcome? At least this card held some promise. The queen of pentacles represented a productive, creative woman, someone who worked hard for her success and prosperity. Home was important to the queen, and so was achieving a balance between reason and imagination. With the queen in this position, Hope saw one possible scenario where Molly's health issues could, if not overcome, at least be managed.

But would that scenario actually happen? Could Molly look forward to recovering from whatever was bothering her? The last card indicated she might not. The five of cups, a card of loss and unhappy endings, showed a figure in a mourning cloak.

"Okay, Molly, so let's start."

Hope was desperate to pull out whatever positive threads she could from the story in front of her. But she couldn't stray *too* far from what the cards seemed to be saying because, after all their years of tarot readings together, Molly had a certain familiarity with the deck, too.

"What I'm seeing here is not all sweetness and light. Maybe you've picked up on that already. But I want to say up front that there are always options for you. In the coming year, you can take charge over how your health situation is handled. You understand what I'm saying?"

Shit! Molly thought. This is already looking bad. Every bit as bad as she thought it might be. And Hope was trying to soften the blow. It was a mistake to agree to this reading.

"Yes, I understand. But I'm getting a weird feeling about it."

Willa sat to one side, watching and listening. She'd been silent up to this point, but now she let out an embarrassed giggle. The reading already felt *so* awkward, even before it actually began. It was like she was eavesdropping on a private and, as it was turning out, unhappy conversation. If she could give the others some crazy excuse and disappear, she would. But where would she go? This was her room too. Besides, she didn't want to make a big deal about leaving just then. It might make things seem even worse.

Hope started by describing the significance of each card, given its place in the Celtic Cross. Then she gave Molly the overarching story.

"Here's the big picture I see from the spread. You're not in one hundred percent perfect health these days..."

That's an understatement if ever I heard one, thought Molly. She nodded but she didn't say anything.

"...But I guess that's pretty much the case for all of us at our age, isn't it?" Hope was searching for comforting words. To Molly, it sounded like Hope's version of 'misery loves company.'

"So let me continue... It looks like your health issues, whatever they may be, might stay with you in the near future."

Molly was tempted to say 'You mean for the rest of my short life,' but that wouldn't help. She knew Hope was already struggling to put the best possible spin on a troubling reading. Why make things more difficult for her? Instead, Molly nodded again.

"The cards are saying you'll need to slow down, take things easy on yourself. Stress will only make things worse. And even after a period of rest, of conserving your energies, you'll likely need more medical care...

"...but here's some good news for a possible path that might be open to you. It's the queen of pentacles here. A strong card. A positive card. It's saying that, under the best circumstances, you will have power over how your health issues are resolved..."

Hope paused. It was true what she said about the queen of pentacles, but the final outcome, if Molly did have some kind of medical problem, wasn't promising.

How could she describe this to Molly?

"...Finally, this last card here tells us about your ultimate prospects. There will continue to be health challenges, but you have many other good things around you to appreciate..."

It was pitiful, Hope knew, her attempt to soften the message. When she tried to catch Molly's eye, Molly looked everywhere except back at her.

Then it hit Hope. Molly was seriously ill, wasn't she? Not just in the early stages of some slow slide toward senility. All the cards pointed to it. They simply reinforced what Hope had observed throughout the weekend.

And Molly already *knew*.

Hope stood up suddenly, almost tipping her chair over backward, and started gathering the cards together.

"Sorry, ladies. I need a break. My head is spinning from all the champagne I've been drinking." Hope didn't want Molly's reading to end like this, especially since it was her birthday, but she was too upset. She had to stop.

Willa finally spoke up.

"Of course. Take as long as you want. Maybe we can do my reading later. Or tomorrow morning, if there's time before we leave." In fact, Willa would be quite happy if Hope didn't read her cards at all.

"Thanks, Willa." Hope was relieved. The way she was feeling, she'd rather not touch the damn tarot cards for a good, long while. Maybe even never again.

Chapter Thirteen

"You sure you can't stay with us a few days, Wills? We've got lots of room and I'd love for us to spend more time together."

Molly and Willa were in their suite, packing their bags in a rush after lingering too long over brunch. Checkout was noon and they were late.

"I'd really like to, but I can't. My boss is expecting me back at work tomorrow morning." Willa closed her suitcase, zipped it up, and shifted it to the floor. Then she sat on her bed waiting for Molly to finish with hers.

"Before we go, Mo, I want to thank you for everything. For inviting me to your big birthday weekend. And for letting me share this gorgeous suite in this amazing resort. I never dreamed I'd get to stay in a place like this..."

Willa paused. She had a lot more to be grateful for.

"...To be honest, I was really anxious about coming back after all this time. I didn't know what to expect. It was good to see you and the others again, of course, but I was worried that I'd be completely overwhelmed by my bad memories. Instead...well...you have *no* idea how much you've helped me, just by listening, and believing me. And thanks for encouraging me to get therapy. It's the right thing to do, of course. It seems so obvious to me now. I owe you big time, Mo."

As Willa spoke, Molly stopped packing, walked over to where she was, and sat beside her.

"You don't owe me anything, Wills. I'm sure you'd do the same for me. And things'll get better for you soon, I promise."

"They're already starting to get better. I can feel it."

Willa checked her watch. She had a plane to catch later that afternoon. "Jesus, Mo. As much as I'd like to stay longer, I don't want to miss my flight. And we should get out of here before they charge you for an extra day."

* * *

How come Molly's so late? Hope wondered. They could be halfway to Ottawa by now.

She was in the lobby, sitting in an armchair facing the elevator, her suitcase to one side. In her opinion, the chair, covered in a brown and orange tapestry pattern, had seen better days. Nervously picking at a loose thread on the arm, she glanced up each time the elevator doors opened and more guests stepped out, then looked away disappointed when Molly wasn't one of them.

Hope had already checked out. All she wanted now was to get back home as soon as she could. Of course, there wasn't much she could do there to make sure

Audrey returned to Ottawa and entered rehab. But it didn't feel right to stay at the resort any longer than absolutely necessary.

Finally, Molly and Willa appeared. Molly went straight to the front desk to settle the bill while Willa joined Hope in the lobby.

"I thought you two would never come down!"

"Sorry if we've made you late...I guess we just lost track of the time."

"It's not so much that I'm late. I'm stressed out about what's happening with Audrey. I'll feel better when I'm home with Gerrit."

"Of course...Before we go, Hope, I want you to know my offer still stands. If your son-in-law needs any help at all in Vancouver, he can give me a call. I can even put him up on my couch if he needs a place to stay."

"Thanks, Willa. That's *so* kind of you. I don't know what's happening with him right now, but I'll text you as soon as I find out more from Gerrit."

Molly finished checking out and wheeled her suitcase over to them.

"Good morning, Hope. I guess that should be 'Good Afternoon.' Sorry to keep you waiting. I seem to be moving slow today. We missed you at brunch...?"

"I decided to have room service." Hope was too anxious that morning to feel sociable and too conscious of her weekend overindulgences to risk further temptation at the buffet. Gerrit wouldn't like it if she started putting on weight.

"Right. Shall we go?"

The three walked together out of the chateau's main entrance and turned left along the drive towards the parking lot, passing the lavish floral displays that seemed so delightfully tropical the day before. It was here that Molly had been inspired to hike through the nature reserve. The idyllic surroundings had the opposite effect on her today.

Her birthday weekend had happy moments, but there were also disappointing ones, not to mention the frightening episode in the woods. Now it was over. And now, each step Molly took away from the chateau brought her closer to reality.

It was difficult saying goodbye as Willa climbed into her rental car with the promise to return for a nice long visit the following spring. Molly, trying to smile, replied with "I'm *so* looking forward to it," but her stomach felt sick as she said it. She figured she'd never see Willa in person again.

Was this what it was going to be like from here on in, she wondered? This desolate feeling that overwhelmed her when someone talked about future plans she might not be around to enjoy?

Her mood didn't improve as they drove away from the chateau, back through the nature reserve and under the resort's arched gateway to reach the main road. For fifteen minutes, neither of them said a word. This isn't like Molly at all, thought Hope. Molly was usually the upbeat one, keeping the conversation bubbling along, no matter what was happening around her. But now she was strangely silent.

"What's the matter, Molly?"

"Oh, I'm okay. Just tired, is all. I'll have a good rest when I get home."

Hope didn't believe her.

"Molly, this is Hope, remember? I know you too well. And what I'm seeing is not tired Molly. It's sad Molly. Even depressed Molly."

She reached over and took Molly's hand.

"There's something wrong, isn't there? Feel like talking about it?" Hope wanted Molly to tell her that, whatever the problem was, it could be fixed. That everything would go back to normal again.

Molly shook her head and started crying.

They had just passed through a village en route to the highway when Hope decided to pull over to the side of the road. That way, she could give Molly her undivided attention. *Saturday In The Park* was playing on the radio and it suddenly seemed rudely loud and upbeat. Hope turned it off and faced Molly.

"Won't you tell me what's going on with you?"

What's the point in holding it in? Molly thought. She's going to find out sooner or later anyway. Likely sooner, if there are any more mishaps like yesterday.

"I'm not well."

Hope waited for her to say more.

"I have cancer. Brain cancer. And it's terminal."

Saying it out loud shocked both of them.

For Molly, even though Gabe knew about her diagnosis, telling someone else made her cancer feel that much closer to an absolute physical fact. It wasn't just some far-off eventuality. It was coming for her. It was going to win and she was going to lose.

As much as Hope knew something was wrong with Molly, she wasn't expecting to hear this. Tears came to her eyes, too. In her mind, she scolded herself. 'Jesus Christ! Just *stop*! Your crying will make things even worse, if that's possible. Molly needs you to be better than this.' She took a deep breath and wiped her eyes with her sleeve.

"Are you sure the doctors can't do something?"

"No, they can't. It's the same cancer that got Gord Downie. And it's going to get me, too. In less than a year."

"Oh my *God*, Molly, this is just so *awful*..."

"I'm sorry, I don't mean to upset you. I really didn't intend to tell anybody this soon, least of all on my birthday weekend."

"Don't be sorry, Molly. I already suspected something wasn't right with you...I hope you're not in pain?"

"Oh, I've had pain. Really horrific headaches. But I've got meds to manage it. And Gabe's making things easier for me, too."

He better be! Hope thought.

"Good. You'll let me know, won't you Molly, if there's anything I can do for you? Call me anytime, day or night, and I'll be there, okay?"

"Of course. Thanks for offering...you're *so* good to me, Hope..."

They sat for a while, still holding hands, before Hope started the car and pulled back out on the road. From there, the drive home took only an hour. Neither of them spoke again until they reached Molly's home.

"Love you so much, girl." Hope helped Molly pull her suitcase out of the trunk of the car and gave her a long hug. "Remember, I'm here whenever you need me. I mean it."

"Thanks, Hope."

Molly made sure to smile at Gabe as she rolled her suitcase up to the front porch where he was waiting.

Chapter Fourteen

It was a perfect evening for dining outdoors at the Canal Grill. There was no hint of rain from the scattered, pink-tinged clouds overhead, their slow easterly progress offering frequent glimpses of a mature sun about to slip behind the far trees. A constant parade of pleasure craft, with passengers lingering on deck to enjoy the balmy air, glided through the canal's rippling blue-grey waves. Only an occasional cool breeze, lifting diners' napkins and ruffling the fringes of patio umbrellas, suggested the approaching end of summer.

For Molly's birthday dinner, Gabe had booked a table close to the water and slightly apart from the others. It was the same one they always asked for when they came to the Grill, their favourite restaurant only ten minutes' walk from home. They ordered their usual dishes too. Linguini con vongole and steak frites.

"So tell me all about your weekend with the girls, Molly."

She had returned from the chateau the day before, but they had yet to talk about her time away. Molly didn't want to raise the topic first. She had her reasons. The main one was that Gabe was undoubtedly still upset she spent her birthday with her friends and not with him. And then there was the fact that the happy getaway she'd hoped for had turned into something less. There had been tense moments, even scary ones. The ones she didn't want Gabe to know about. But now that he'd asked, she'd select a few highlights.

"Well, it was *so* nice to see everybody again and catch up. And the chateau was simply spectacular. The food was amazing, and we all ate too much. We spent Saturday afternoon at the spa and it was wonderful, too. *So* relaxing. I felt really spoiled."

The server arrived then with their entrees. For Molly, it was perfect timing. She'd run out of positive things to say. And, after a lot of reflection, she'd decided not to mention her exchange with Beth at the marina, or tease out Gabe's reaction to it. What would be the point, after all? He'd only deny it, just like Beth did. It would be a tough conversation she really didn't need.

"So, did you have some kind of special dinner? Birthday cake and all that?"

Gabe worked through his fifteen chews of steak while she decided how much she wanted to say, and then answered.

"Yes, it was lovely. Just the three of us. But nothing over the top...we ordered room service. And Hope did a tarot reading after."

"Oh? And what about those marijuana cigarettes you took with you?"

"We shared one on the beach right after our spa treatments. Too bad Beth had a reaction to the smoke. A touch of asthma. She got over it pretty fast, but it wasn't a good idea to bring out the others...And before we left, I hid a second one in Willa's suitcase, just for fun. She's probably found it by now. I still have the third one, if you want to try it with me sometime."

Not surprisingly, Gabe shook his head.

Molly hesitated, then looked Gabe in the eye.

"I never knew Beth had asthma. Did you?"

It was as close as Molly wanted to get to raising the spectre of their affair. Maybe she shouldn't even have gone that far, but she couldn't resist.

The question clearly annoyed Gabe.

"No. Of course not. What a strange thing to ask! Why would I?"

He vigorously sawed off another piece of steak, thrust it in his mouth, and started chewing again.

Molly didn't answer. She just shrugged and let it go.

"I've been doing a lot of thinking, Gabe...you know...about my cancer."

"Do we need to talk about this tonight, Molly? We're having such a nice evening."

They'd finished dinner and were strolling along the canal, taking the long way home. They were even holding hands, something they hadn't done in years.

"I know. But indulge me just for a moment. It's important."

"All right."

"Okay, so as I said, I've been thinking how things will go for me...for us...over the coming months. We both know it's going to get worse. The headaches. The nausea. The memory lapses. I haven't had any other symptoms yet, but who knows?

"I really don't want to keep dealing with all this. And, for sure, I don't want to put you through it either. Or the kids."

"But Molly..."

"I know what you're going to say. You're going to say you can handle it. And you'll be there for me. Well, I'm grateful for that. *Very* grateful. But why let this damn cancer make things *so* difficult for us?"

Gabe stopped abruptly and frowned as he turned to face her. It was hard to tell whether he was about to cry or get angry. Maybe both, Molly thought, from the grim look on his face.

"Where the hell are you going with this Molly? What are you suggesting?"

"I'm not exactly sure. But I want the pain to stop. I want to make this as easy as possible. For me *and* you. I'd like to find out more about the 'medical assistance in dying' thing we've been hearing about. MAID, they call it. I've seen some articles about it in the newspaper. I don't know how it works, or if it even applies to me. But if it ends the misery, and I can decide when and where to do it, then that's what I want."

"Why not try surgery instead, like the doctor suggested? And radiation? Chemotherapy? Or have you dismissed all that?"

"I'm not sure how much they'd improve things. And they won't give me much more time anyway. That's what the doctor told us, remember?"

"Yes, I remember. I'm *really* not comfortable with what you're saying, Molly. But I suppose how I feel about it doesn't matter, does it?"

"Of course, it matters, Gabe! That's why I wanted to talk to you about it."

"Well, it sounds like you've pretty much made up your mind already."

"I guess I have. If it's available to me."

"So, then, where do *I* fit in the equation?"

"Believe me, Gabe, I'm thinking this would be the best thing for you, too. I'm convinced MAID would make it easier for *both* of us."

From the sour look on Gabe's face, Molly could tell he didn't agree.

"Let me do some digging and we can talk about this again, once I know a little bit more about it, okay?"

"If you must. But Molly, I don't want to lose you. I want us to be together as long as possible."

A single tear rolled down Gabe's cheek. Molly reached up and wiped it away.

They'd had more than forty years and a family together. Some of that time was good, some not so good. Long ago, Molly had realized they weren't soulmates,

Gabe and she. But they *had* been life mates. Since the late seventies, neither of them had ever lived without the other. Gabe wasn't angry. He was afraid. She understood that now. Because she was afraid too.

"I know. I feel the same."

She took his arm and they started walking again.

"Let's have a nice coffee and a liqueur when we get home, okay, Gabe?"

Gabe nodded. He was too upset to speak.

Chapter Fifteen

Molly made up her mind the day after Thanksgiving.

She'd had the whole family over dinner. Turkey and stuffing and roast vegetables and pumpkin pie. All the traditional dishes. For Molly, taking it slow this time, the usual two-day major production turned into almost three days. She fully expected to be exhausted by the time they all sat down at the table, and she was. What she didn't expect was her total loss of appetite. Instead, while the others dug in, Molly toyed with her minted peas, pushing them around the plate and under a mound of mashed potato. Then she cut her slice of turkey breast into a dozen tiny pieces and covered them all with gravy, hoping that, if she looked busy, nobody would notice she wasn't actually eating anything. They didn't.

Every other aspect of their dinner was unremarkable. The talk around the table was the same as it always was, ranging from politics to sports to the latest on Netflix. When Cam had a little too much to drink, and the volume of his pronouncements on the state of the world grew louder with each glass of wine he consumed, nobody was surprised. As usual, Carrie's two young ones were excused early from the table to go play computer games. And this time, Molly didn't forget Jeremy's name. Funny how such a mundane accomplishment felt like a big win.

But after everybody left, and she was putting the last dishes in the dishwasher, Molly blacked out. She crashed to the floor, her unseeing eyes fluttering open and closed and her muscles first going rigid, then limp. The seizure didn't last long. Gabe was there to help her get up again, shuffle to the living room, and lie on the couch.

"I'm calling an ambulance. Or I'll take you to emergency myself."

"NO! I'm better now. Just...want...to sleep."

"I don't agree, Molly. You need help. Now."

"Not...going...anywhere."

He heard the edge in her voice and gave up. Upsetting Molly in her current state wasn't a good idea.

"Have it your way, but I'm calling the doctor first thing in the morning."

"If...you...insist," Molly whispered, before turning on her side and closing her eyes. An hour later, Gabe helped her climb the stairs to their bedroom.

She woke up at 6 am. Ever so carefully, she swung her legs over the side of the bed and pushed herself to her feet. For a few seconds, all she could see was a grey blur as a jolt of pain flashed through her head. Swaying slightly before finding her balance, she didn't dare move for fear of falling again.

When Molly's vision cleared, she walked slowly to the bathroom, her hand reaching for the wall to steady herself on the way. She switched on the light and went to the mirror to inspect the damage from her fall. One side of her face was swollen and bruised from striking the edge of the dishwasher door as she went down. Her left shoulder ached, and it had bruising too. It must have been the first part of her that hit the floor. Red-rimmed eyes, staring back at her, reflected her exhaustion. And her anger. Anger because, for months, she'd been betrayed by her own body. How could she *not* feel insulted by the pain that kept getting worse? How could she *ever* accept the humiliation from her mental lapses?

She didn't need this. She *really* didn't need this. She was a hazard to herself and a burden to Gabe. And it was never going to get better. So, yes, Gabe could call Doctor Flanagan. He could make her an appointment and take her to it. And when she got there, she was going to ask for medical assistance in dying. Gabe wasn't going to like it. Not one bit. But Molly knew better. It was the best thing for them both, even if he refused to admit it.

* * *

Dr. Flanagan saw them at the end of the afternoon that same day.

"I really don't want to live like this, doctor. I can't do *anything*... I can't drive... I have no appetite... And sometimes I think I'm losing my mind... the headaches...the dizzy spells I've been having ...well...what if I have one on our stairs? ...or in public somewhere? I just can't *stand* it anymore."

The words came out slow. It was a major effort for Molly to say even this much.

"I'm sorry to hear about this, Molly. Are you taking the painkillers I prescribed? And should we go ahead with your treatment plan? We might have to make adjustments, of course. I hate to say it, but the tumour might have progressed somewhat since your diagnosis in August..."

"NO! I don't want ANY of that. No surgery... no radiation... none...of...that stuff. I know I'm terminal...no matter what...you do. I want to go easy...on my terms...and I'm ready. Can you help me?"

"You're talking about medical assistance in dying?"

"Yes."

Gabe sat slumped in the chair facing Dr. Flanagan, looking down at the floor. Except for the almost imperceptible shaking of his head, he didn't move most of the time she was talking. Toward the end, when Molly said, "I'm ready," his whole body shuddered. Then he looked sideways at her, and she looked back at him. She could see he wasn't happy. But there was a hint of something else in his half-shut eyes. He always had that look when he resented something she said or did.

It wasn't her fault, what was happening to her. She'd do anything to make the cancer go away. But that wasn't going to happen. Surely, he wouldn't want her to keep suffering. What she wanted was really the only logical option, wasn't it?

Dr. Flanagan could see Gabe was upset, too.

"I know this is difficult for the two of you. How about I go over how the process works? I've helped guide a couple of my patients through MAID, so I'm familiar with it. Then you can take some time to reflect on this a bit more together and come back with your decision, okay?"

"Okay," Molly answered. She already knew it was what she wanted. Maybe if Gabe learned more about it, he would come around to her way of thinking.

"Give me a minute to pull up the MAID information, just to be sure I don't skip anything." Dr. Flanagan turned to her desktop computer and searched for the website. Once it was opened, she looked back at Molly and Gabe.

"Well, the first thing you should know is that MAID can only be offered in cases where the medical condition is serious. The words they use for that are 'grievous and irremediable.'"

She scrolled down then continued.

"The assessment as to whether a person qualifies takes into account whether the illness is incurable and causes suffering, either mental or physical, that can't be relieved. And it's not just one doctor's assessment, but two."

Molly was already nodding when the doctor looked up again, then back down at the screen.

"You would need to give formal written consent to the procedure, but, before you do, I'm required to give you full details on counselling services, mental health and disability support, community services, and palliative care, in addition to MAID. I would offer to arrange consultations with professionals for these services." Dr.

Flanagan paused. "Am I being clear so far? Let me know if you have any questions at all."

Gabe didn't say anything. He had no questions. For him, it was already too much information. Only Molly responded.

"Yes...very clear...no questions yet."

"Okay. Now. About consent. As I said, it has to be in writing. It must be voluntary and it must be witnessed by an independent party. It can be withdrawn at any time, right up until the point the final medication is administered."

"What do I need to say...in my written consent?"

"Don't worry about that now. And there's a standard request form I could give you.

"As far as the timeline goes, there's a waiting period after a request is approved, depending on the capacity to give consent. Could be ninety days, could be less. Once the waiting period is over, either a doctor can administer the dose, or the patient can do it with a doctor present. And it would take place in a setting of the patient's choice."

The doctor closed the website and turned back to face them.

"So, that's just a quick overview. I hope it helps. The general idea is that, if it's approved, you would have total control at every stage as to whether MAID should or should not proceed. I can email you some links that go into a lot more detail. You'll see that the process can be adjusted, depending on each patient's particular circumstances."

"Thank you, doctor...Thanks for the explanation." Molly turned to Gabe. "What do you think?"

"I don't know *what* to think at this point."

Dr. Flanagan and Molly exchanged glances.

"Of course, it's a lot to absorb. Take as long as you need. Let me know."

* * *

The following Monday was a good day for Molly. There was no crushing headache when she got out of bed, and navigating the stairs on her own was easier than it had been for a while. In the kitchen, she poured coffee into a mug and brought it over to the table where Gabe, reading the Globe and Mail, had just finished his toast. He reached over and pulled out the chair beside him so she could settle into it more easily.

"Morning, Molly. You sleep okay?"

"Yes, for once. And I'm feeling much better this morning."

"Great!"

Molly took a sip from her mug. Her mind was clear, as clear as it ever had been, even before the cancer. She needed it to be, because it was time to deal with what was to come. Their conversation about MAID was unfinished. They'd each heard the facts from Dr. Flanagan. They'd each had time to think about it since. What was the point of putting it off any longer?

"Can we talk about my situation now, Gabe? It's important."

"Your situation?"

His answer, or rather his question, was *so* irritating. Gabe knew what she meant. Why was he being deliberately obtuse? It just made this so much harder.

"You know what I'm talking about. MAID, of course. What the doctor described last week."

Gabe folded the newspaper, set it aside, stood up, and started pacing. So this was going to be it. 'The Talk.' He knew it was coming, just not so soon. He wasn't ready for it. When would he ever be?

"You really want to get into this now, Molly? And besides, what's there to say? You've already made up your mind, right?"

"Well, basically, yes. But I think it's important...you understand me...that we understand each other."

"Okay. So?"

"So let me start... I've thought a lot about this, Gabe. And here's what I want you to know. I've had sixty-five years on this planet, most of them spent with you. We've had two great kids together. And even though we've had some bad spells, I've always tried to be a good wife to you. You've been there for me, too, when it counted.

"We're best friends, aren't we, Gabe, after all we've been through? And, if I didn't have this damn tumour in my head...we could have had many *more* years together.

We could have watched our grandkids grow up...we could have travelled...gone to concerts...had fun with our friends. All those things. But, for me, none of that is going to happen. Because I'll be gone this time next year. And we have to face that fact. Together."

As good as she was feeling, it was hard for Molly to get all the words out. So many sentences. Taking so long. And she wasn't done.

Gabe dropped back down into his seat.

"Molly, I..."

"No! Just let me finish, Gabe. Then I'll listen...to everything you have to say."

"Go ahead."

"I have a death sentence. There's no other way to say it. And I have a choice. I can either go in pain...losing my mind a little bit more every day...for God knows how long...a bother to you in every way...or I can choose my time and place...and go with whatever's left of my dignity."

Molly moved her chair closer to Gabe, took his hands, and looked into his eyes.

"It's not that I want to leave *you,* Gabe. It's that I want to leave *me*. The 'me' that can't function anymore...the 'me' that can't think for myself...or do things for myself. I've always been independent...and I can't stand giving that up...I hate what's coming, Gabe...what's actually already here. So *please* try to understand...why I want to do this. Can you do that?"

Gabe nodded. "Of course, I understand. I understand every word you're saying. I'm just having a hard time accepting it.

"Maybe I'm being selfish, Molly. But to be honest, I don't know how I'm going to live after you're...you know...gone. It feels like the end for me, too. I think 'why does she want to leave me any earlier than she has to?'...and, of course, I already know the answer to that. It's the pain. I can see it's getting worse... so, I get what you want to do. And why. And, as much as I have a hard time with it, I will support you."

"Thanks, Gabe...that's such a relief."

Gabe shrugged his shoulders in defeat. Did Molly have any idea how much of a concession this was on his part?

"So, I guess the next step is we go back to the doctor?"

"Yes. But Gabe, before we do, we need to decide on a few things, you and me."

"Okay?"

"First, we need to tell Cam and Carrie about the cancer...and I think we should do it soon. They might already be wondering...what's going on with me. Then, from what the doctor said...I'll need to go through the MAID assessment. If it's approved...and I hope to God it *is*...I'd like to spend one last Christmas with the family. After that, I want it to happen in January. Here, in our home. How do you feel about all this?"

"God, Molly! That's only three months from now. But if that's your decision..."

"It is."

Gabe reached for Molly and they held on to each other.

"You talked about our bad spells, Molly. I'll take the blame for that. I *do* love you, you know, in my own strange way. I always have, ever since university. But I know I haven't been the husband you deserved. I don't want to get into all of that now. All I can say is I'm sorry. I truly am." He tilted his head to one side. "How've you been able to put up with me all these years?"

Gabe wasn't the type who used the word 'love' very often. And he rarely apologized for anything. For him, saying these things was a major concession.

Molly touched his cheek. It was her way of showing she forgave him. Then she smiled.

"Beats me!"

Chapter Sixteen

"Happy New Year, Hope!"

They had to resort to Zooming again. Molly hated it. This wasn't the way she wanted to have her last conversation with an old friend. But the Omicron variant, exploding throughout the city over the holidays, put a stop to their plans to get together in person.

"And to you, Molly."

It was a strange thing to say, and Hope knew it, but the words just slipped out. Obviously, 2022 was *not* going to be a happy year for Molly.

"You and Gerrit have a good Christmas?"

"It was wonderful. Audrey and Arjun and Ravi spent Christmas Day with us. It was so nice to see them all together again."

"And everybody's well?"

Molly was curious about Audrey's progress. She'd heard in October that her goddaughter was in rehab, but she didn't want to ask about it directly. Hope figured out that was what she meant anyway.

"Yes. Everybody. It was such a relief to see Audrey looking healthy. Almost like her old self again. She tells me she's off the painkillers. Did it cold turkey. I know it's been rough for her, but so far, she seems to be sticking with it. And she and Arjun are getting along so much better these days. I'm keeping my fingers crossed for them."

"That's *such* good news, Hope. I'm glad for you."

"And you, Molly? How was Christmas with the kids?"

"It was wonderful. We all went to...Carrie's place for dinner...I'm not up to...cooking big meals...any meals...these days."

Hope noticed how slow and deliberate Molly's words came out. It was clearly an effort for her to say even this much.

"So how are you feeling now, Molly? I hope you're not suffering..."

"Well, that's why I called...the pain's not letting up...and I'm sick and tired of it. I don't mean to depress you, Hope... but I have to tell you...I just don't want to do it anymore..."

"What does that mean?"

"It means I've decided it's my time to go. Have you heard about...medical assistance in dying?"

"Yes. I've read about it. You're thinking of doing *that*?!...You sure, Molly???"

"Yes. I'm sure. There's no doubt in my mind. It's all been arranged...for the week after next...just Gabe and the kids will be with me."

"Oh my God, Molly, I'm *so, so* sorry..."

"Don't be sorry. To me, it feels...absolutely right...to do it this way. It's actually a big relief...to know the craziness will finally stop...and I can leave on my terms...in my own home."

"You're sounding very calm about it."

"I am...I'm *totally* at peace with this, Hope...To me, this is the best way to go...the *only* way I want to go."

"You're such a strong woman, Molly. You always have been. I admire you so much for that."

"Thank you."

"Have you told the others? Willa and Beth, I mean?"

"No, not yet."

"Do you want me to do it? Would that make it easier for you?" Hope had no problem contacting Willa. As for Beth, she'd force herself to call her if that's what Molly wanted.

"I'll tell Willa myself."

"And Beth?"

Molly remembered the coldness between Hope and Beth during her birthday weekend, and she knew they wouldn't be having a cordial conversation. But it would be at least as hard for her to do it herself. On top of everything else Molly was going through, she didn't need the extra grief.

"How do you feel...about talking to her?"

"For you, I'll do it."

"Thanks, Hope. I know it's a big favour."

There wasn't a lot more to say. They sat looking fondly at each other for a few final moments. Molly could see tears in Hope's eyes.

"I'm going to miss you so much, Molly! I wish I could give you a big hug right now!"

"I know...me too...but I'll see you on the other side. So let's not say goodbye. When it's your turn...bring your cards with you. Maybe we can do...a tarot reading up there..."

Molly's attempt to lighten things up didn't work. Hope started to cry.

"I love you, Molly."

"I love you too, Hope."

Molly had to lie down for an hour before Zooming Willa. She was completely exhausted. Saying goodbye to Hope had been *so* difficult. And it would likely be worse with Willa, who didn't even know about the cancer.

The second Molly's face appeared on her screen, Willa knew she was ill. The spark in her eyes was gone and she'd lost a lot of weight.

The first thing they did was exchange New Year's greetings. It was early January after all. But Willa couldn't help commenting about Molly's appearance after that.

"You're looking a little pale, Mo. You okay?"

"No. Not really..."

Then Molly, in halting sentences, told Willa about the cancer, and about her decision to end things her way. Willa, like Hope, wasn't able to hold back her tears.

"Oh my *God,* Mo, this is such a *shock*!"

"I know...I'm sorry...to be giving you such shitty news...but I couldn't put it off any longer. Would it help you to know...that I feel completely...comfortable doing this?"

"I guess so. Maybe a little. But it's just *so* unfair. This shouldn't be happening to *you,* of all people..."

"I used to think that way, Wills...but it really shouldn't happen...to anyone, should it? I just have to accept it. And I do."

"I don't know what more to say, Mo, except thank you for being my friend. Because of you, I'm doing *so* much better these days. I'll never forget what you've given me..."

"I'm glad, Wills."

"Should I come to Ottawa? Could I be of any help at all to you and Gabe? Sit with you? Keep you company? Maybe run some errands?"

"Nice of you to offer, Wills. And I'd love to see you in person. But we're managing okay. And besides, with this damn Omicron, people aren't supposed to travel, are they?"

"I guess not..."

"I'm sorry Wills, I have to go lie down for a bit. I'm feeling a little lightheaded."

It was true, how Molly was feeling, but she also wanted to say goodbye to Willa now, before she started crying too.

"Of course, Mo. But let me say I think it takes *so* much courage to do what you're doing."

"Thanks, Wills...I love you."

"And I'll always love you."

Molly hung up quickly.

Willa was right. It wasn't fair.

Molly hadn't really cried about what was happening to her since she first told Hope on the way home from their weekend getaway at the resort. Now she climbed into bed, curled herself around a pillow, and gave in to the hurt.

For months, she'd tried to be stronger than the cancer, hadn't she? Despite the pain, she'd carried on like it wasn't such a big deal. She'd celebrated her birthday in style with the girls. She'd managed to hold it together at Thanksgiving and over the Christmas holidays for the sake of Gabe and Cam and Carrie and the grandkids. For them, she did her best to act almost normal. To show calm acceptance. No wonder they all thought she was so strong.

She made sure they saw no traces in her of the stages of grief everybody talked about. The denial. The anger. The depression. But they were there, inside her all along, making only brief appearances in the five months since her diagnosis. And now they were bearing down on her, crushing her, all at once.

It was the last time she cried.

She was asleep when Gabe found her. He covered her with the old cashmere throw and went downstairs to eat his dinner by himself. It was something he'd have to get used to.

Molly slept soundly through the night. When she woke up, the wave of deep desolation she'd felt the previous afternoon had passed. She felt surprisingly calm. Refreshed, even. It was inevitable, she thought, that the blackness would catch up with her and roll over her at some point. Thank God, it didn't stay long. It might come back in the few days she had left, of course, but she knew she could handle it. And what else – or who else – could possibly hurt her now, anyway?

* * *

"Molly...it's...Beth."

They hadn't talked since Molly's birthday when Beth left the chateau early. Her words were hesitant. She wasn't sure how Molly would react when she heard her voice. She needn't have worried.

"Beth! Happy New Year!"

Molly could imagine Beth's relief at the other end.

"Thanks, Molly...Hope called me last evening. She told me all about what's happening with you. Such *terrible* news. I can hardly believe it...I hope you're comfortable at least?"

"Yes. I've had my rough spells. But...most of the time...it's bearable."

"Good. Can I do anything for you? Bring you anything?"

"Thanks, but no. It's not necessary. I have...everything I need." Besides, it wouldn't be a good idea for Beth to come over when Gabe was there.

"Molly, I'll miss you. You've always been so good to me."

I wish I could say the same about you, Molly thought. But it really doesn't matter anymore.

"I know, Beth. We had fun over the years, didn't we?"

"Yes. Lots of fun."

There wasn't much else Molly wanted to say.

"Well...thanks for getting in touch, Beth."

It was her way to end the call.

"It's the least I could do. 'Bye, Molly...Love you."

At the last second, Molly whispered into the phone.

"Beth...I want you to know...I forgive you."

Then she hung up.

Molly didn't know how long those words were waiting to come out. And was it true, what she said? Did she really mean it? With all the mixed-up thoughts colliding in her head these days, she wasn't exactly sure. But she felt better for saying it. A parting gift, she realized. To Beth. And to herself.

Chapter Seventeen

The fifth of August. It would have been his and Molly's forty-fourth wedding anniversary. A glass of scotch in his hand, Gabe sat alone on the back deck looking out over the kitchen garden that, for years, had been Molly's big summer project. He recognized the chives, the asparagus, the rhubarb. This year, something else was thriving there, too, and it seemed to be choking out the rest. With its frilly greenish-purple leaves, it looked disgustingly healthy. Maybe one of those so-called "superfoods", jam-packed with nutrients, that came into vogue for a year or two until the next trendy edible showed up on restaurant menus. He didn't have a clue what it was, and he didn't care.

Gabe had let the garden run wild this season. Too much mucking about in the soil on one's hands and knees as far as he was concerned. His role in property maintenance had always been limited to mowing the lawn, front and back, and he did it with a frequency and precision that had Molly accusing him of having OCD.

Maybe he *had* been a bit obsessive about it, but it was important to keep the place looking good, wasn't it? And now, even more so. Soon, it was going up for sale. Everything would have to look absolutely perfect, inside and out. He might even have to wade into Molly's overgrown kitchen garden and tidy that up, too. A major pain in the ass, given the months of his neglect.

The house was way too big for him these days. The only time he felt the slightest bit comfortable in it since Molly's death in January was when family visited, and *that* didn't happen very often. You reap what you sow, Gabe acknowledged, every time he'd invite them over and they declined. 'Prior commitments' was always the excuse. He'd been a hands-off father, and now he had too-busy kids and grandkids. Served him right.

'You don't know what you got till it's gone.' How many times had that unwelcome earworm from an old Joni Mitchell song played over and over in his head? It was exactly how he felt, though. Bereft of human contact for days on end. The crushing stillness, the sense that he barely existed – to the whole world, let alone to his children – was relentless. The worst times were in the mornings, before he went downstairs to fix himself breakfast, when he couldn't think of a single good reason to get out of bed. A reluctant hermit, he had to keep the three TVs in the house turned on all day to drown out the stifling silence. In the kitchen, Alexa, with her bad jokes and weather updates and medication reminders, became his new best friend.

He knew he'd be lonely after Molly passed, but nothing had prepared him for such profound isolation.

And what was worse, he was surrounded by all the things she left behind. Everywhere he turned there were knickknacks and plants and books and so much more she'd accumulated over four decades, all taking turns to ambush him. It was a true act of mercy that, the week after Molly's death, Carrie had bagged her clothes and left them on the doorstep for the Diabetes van to pick up. It would have been unbearable torture to tackle that himself.

The loneliness and the physical reminders were bad enough. Over time, he might have been able to deal with both. But there was one big obstacle he knew he would never overcome. Molly had chosen their bedroom as the place where she wanted to die. He understood why, but Gabe hadn't been able to sleep in that room, in that bed, ever since. He moved his clothes across the hall to Cam's old bedroom and slept there instead. After six months of this, he'd had enough. At the end of July, he made the decision to put the house on the market.

Thinking back to that frigid January evening, he could only admire how well Molly had organized her own passing. It was timed perfectly, at just after five o'clock, so she could watch the sunset through the frost-framed bedroom window. First, Gabe lit the lavender-scented candles Molly had asked him to place around the room earlier, casting a warm golden glow over what was about to unfold. Then he helped her put on her favourite fleece outfit and settle on the bed. After he'd covered her with her grandmother's quilt, he and Cam and Carrie whispered their final goodbyes. Gabe held Molly's hand as her children stepped back. "I'm ready. You have my final consent." Molly said the words firmly so there could be no doubt. Dr. Flanagan did the rest.

Then, in the intimacy of the moment, they shared the sad privilege of witnessing Molly's last breaths. *Into The Mystic* was playing in the background when she finally slipped away. There were quiet tears, but there was no wailing. No drama at all. For Gabe, it was because he finally felt reconciled to her departure. For them all, there was relief in the placid manner of her leaving.

It was *so* very Molly. Gabe had to admit that, as far as deaths go, it was a good one.

He took a last sip of scotch, carried the empty glass back to the kitchen, and put it in the dishwasher. In the living room, he walked over to the fireplace and opened a carved wooden box on the mantel. It was from the '70's. A wedding gift, he seemed to recall. He'd found the last of Molly's marijuana cigarettes in the box right after her death. Gabe actually meant to throw it out at some point, but now he was glad he didn't. He wasn't exactly sure why, but he somehow felt he owed it to Molly to celebrate their anniversary with it. Most likely, it was stale – she'd bought it a whole year earlier, after all – but he took it out of the box anyway and went to the pantry off the kitchen where they kept the matches. Returning to his chair on the deck, he inhaled deeply as he lit the cigarette. Then he exhaled and raised it in a salute.

"Here's to you, Molly! Happy Anniversary, my girl!"

When it was burned halfway down, he decided he'd had enough and butted it out. By then, he was a little bit drunk and a little bit stoned. That made it easier for what he planned to do next. Reaching for his cellphone, he scrolled through his contacts list for a number he used to know well, but now couldn't remember. There was no answer when he called, so he left a voice message instead.

"Hi, Beth. It's Gabe Bustin. Long time no speak, I know. But I wonder if you might come over at some point in the next few days? I've decided to put the house on the market, and I thought you might be interested in handling the sale for me. Call me back, okay? And maybe we can crack open a bottle of wine while you're here."

About the Author

Anna Blauveldt was born and raised in Fredericton, New Brunswick, and graduated with an Honours B.A. degree from the University of New Brunswick. She then moved to Ottawa to join the federal government and was honoured to be appointed Canada's Ambassador to Iceland before leaving to pursue her next career as an author.

She subsequently completed the Post-Graduate Creative Writing Program of Humber College, Toronto and obtained an M.A. degree with Merit in Creative and Critical Writing from the University of Gloucestershire, UK, in 2019.

Published works include,

- "Kat and the Meanies" – 2022, Broken Keys Publishing & Press
- "Irma" - 2019 anthology 'A Two-Four of Tales', Ottawa Independent Writers
- "Released" - 2020 anthology 'Short Stories for a Long Year', Ottawa Independent Writers
- "BFF" - 2022 anthology 'Conversations', Unleash Press (Ohio USA)
- "Harvest Festival" - 2022 anthology 'Ghosts and Other Cthonic Macabres,' Broken Keys Publishing & Press.
- "To Play At God" and "Ask Gloria" - Published in one volume, October 2021, Publerati, (Maine USA).

Also available from Broken Keys Publishing

Symphonies of Horror:
Inspirational Tales by H. P. Lovecraft: The Symbiot Appendum

Thin Places: The Ottawan Anthology
(Winner of the Faces of Ottawa 2021 Book of the Year Award)

Love & Catastrophé Poetré
(Winner of the Faces of Ottawa 2022 Book of the Year Award)

Ghosts and Other Chthonic Macabres

Sadness of the Siren, *by Samantha Underhill*

Missing the Exit, *by Michael Adubato*

Little Dragon, *by Jana Begovic*
Poisonous Whispers, *by Jana Begovic*

Kat and the Meanies, *by Anna Blauveldt*

Titles by Michel Weatherall:
The Symbiot 30th Anniversary: The Nadia Edition
Necropolis
The Refuse Chronicles
The Symbiot Trilogy Box-Set
Ngaro's Sojourney
A Dark Corner of My Soul

www.brokenkeyspublishing.com

CPSIA information can be obtained
at www.ICGtesting.com
Printed in the USA
LVHW101540181122
733278LV00018B/891

9 798215 361467